Published 2024 by Severnside Books
All enquiries to Severnside Books, 44 York St Cardiff CF5 1NE
Or to jonblakeauthor@gmail.com

ISBN 978-1-9168775-1-1

A CIP catalogue record of this book is available from the British Library.

Cover design by Jon and Zazie Blake.

Jon Blake is the author of over sixty titles for children, young adults and adults, including the half million selling picture book *You're a Hero Daley B.* He is a BBC Talent award winner for radio comedy and has been shortlisted for the Children's Book Award, the Laugh Out Loud Awards and the Writers Guild Best Children's TV Script, while his YA novel *The Last Free Cat* was chosen by the International Literary Association for their prestigious Young Choices list. Brought up in Southampton, he wrote his first novel in York, teacher trained in Barnsley, became a professional author and playwright in Nottingham and moved to Cardiff in 1987, where he now lives with Natalie, their two children and Flora the cat. His books website is at www.jonblake.co.uk and his tutoring website is at www.parkwrite.com.

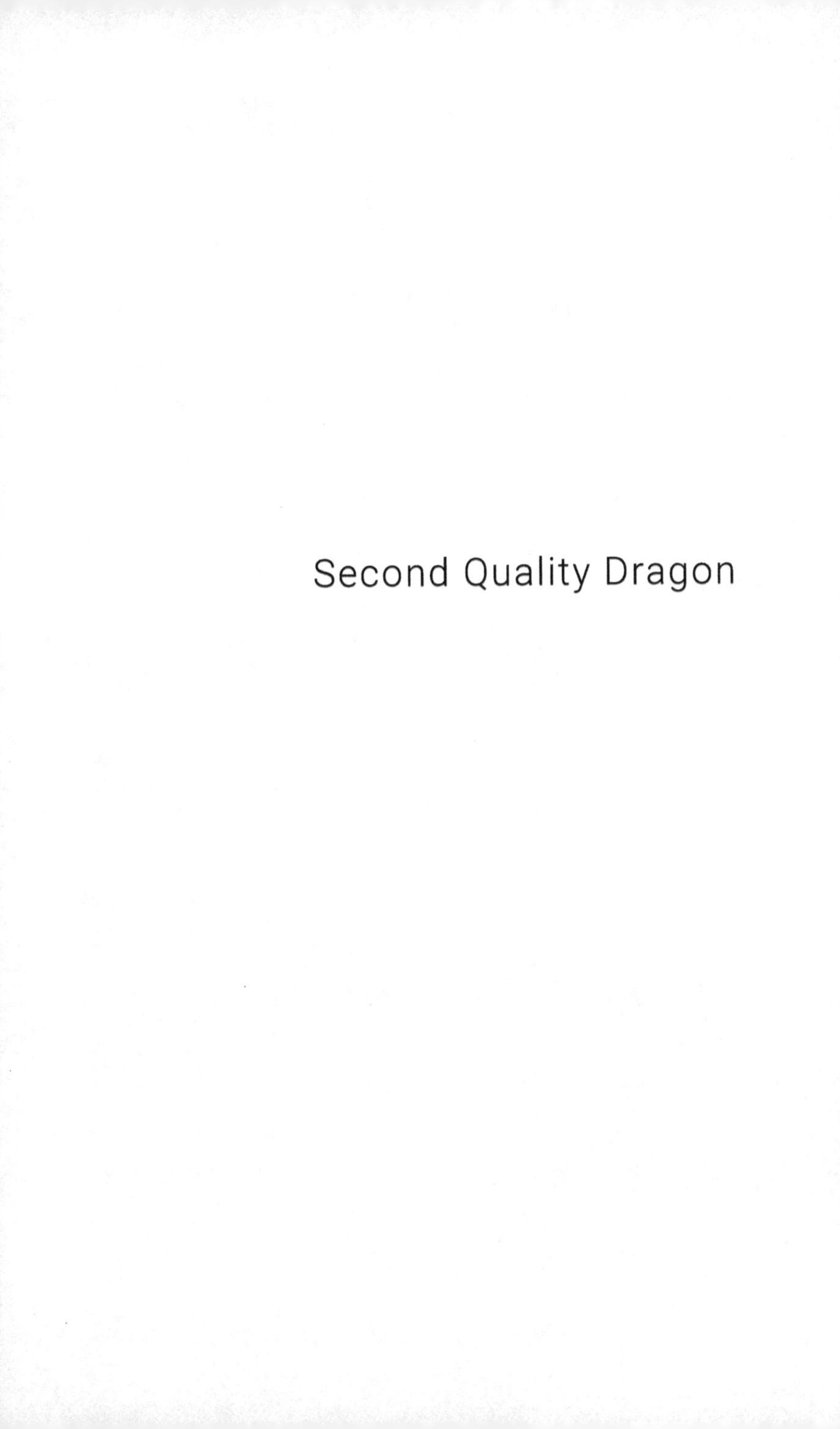

Second Quality Dragon

Second Quality Dragon

Jon Blake

Clapton's truck came hissing and whirring down the streets of Llantresedd, past the tourist information centre and the Glyndwr Hotel, along Ruby Street with its Dekker Dragon Megastore, downhill to Eastgate with its cafes and old market cross, and finally along that narrow low-lying backstreet known as Toadstool Lane. Here were nothing but grey terrace houses, a memorial masons specialising in marble gravestones, and opposite that a converted sweet shop now known as the Bargain Dragons Centre.

A young teenage girl propped open the front door of this store. She knew what Clapton was bringing, she didn't like it, but she was not about to complain. Caron had messed up at school through her stubborn refusal to do what she was told, and for reasons which will become clear, was hanging on to her new job for grim death.

"Morning," said Clapton. The hard-faced little man rarely said more. Caron helped him unload the first of the cages from the back of the van.

"Bring on the babies!" Dav, the shop manager, liked to treat everything as a joke, but he knew as well as anybody that Clapton's dragons were not babies, but pitifully small and weak creatures, some blind, some without colour, all second quality. The few that had shiny scales went into the window display, the rest back in the long, narrow showroom alongside the dragon food and the breath converters. These breath converters were supposed to store the warmth that the dragons gave off, but all the sales staff knew they were virtually useless, nothing like the machines in the Ruby Street store which could heat a mansion.

Dav paid off Clapton, then set about inspecting the new stock. For this task he was joined by the second junior seller, known as Dobbin for his donkey-like braying laugh. Unlike Caron, Dobbin was ideally suited to his job, his head like a swivelling gun turret with narrow calculating eyes. Dav and Dobbin liked to label their hopeless dragons with ridiculously glorious names such as Inferno and Genghis Khan. But actually feeling something for these sad specimens was strictly out of order.

"Better leave the window as it is" said Dav. "This lot are fit for the knackers yard".

Caron and Dobbin duly carried the cages to the far end of the shop while Dav wrote out the price tags. The dragons were a fraction of the price of the gleaming monsters up on Ruby Street, and as the sellers got five per cent of each sale and precious little else, their pay was as pitiful as the pale whimpering creatures they sold. But as the big boss owned houses as well as shops, they got a flat along with the job, one of the reasons why Caron had to toe the line at all costs.

There was also the possibility of promotion. Many of the sellers on Ruby Street had started out on Toadstool Lane. If Jac Dekker took a shine to you your pay could rise tenfold, and your two-room flat could be swapped for a penthouse. How Caron would have loved that, a luxury crib to which she could invite her dad, the man who'd called her a waster and thrown her out of her childhood home.

Caron's dad was never far from her thoughts during times like these, when there were no customers and memories of her recent past threatened to overwhelm her. But today, as she attached the price tags to the new dragons, something unexpected attracted her attention. One of the new dragons was looking at her.

It might not seem unusual, to be looked at by one of these creatures, but it was actually rarer than hen's teeth. The one thing that united this ragbag of dismal dragons was their total lack of interest in the world around them. They were aware of the pellets put into their feeders, but other than that their lives consisted of scratching themselves, restlessly pacing, or sleeping. A face pressed up to their bars meant nothing. Loud conversation was ignored. They expected nothing, so reacted to nothing.

So, what was it about this dragon? It did have some colour, unlike most of the others. But, oh dear, its right wing was withered and hung limply by its side. Even if it got out of its cage it could never fly.

Did that have something to do with its interest in her, as she walked so freely before its cage? But Dobbin and Dav were both moving about within its eyesight, yet it did not glance once towards them.

"Caz!"

Caron looked up. Dav was waving furiously.

"Look lively, Caz, it's the dynamic duo!"

Caron felt a familiar sinking feeling. Two strutting figures had entered the shop, as they did every Monday. One a lumbering giant with ferocious eyes, the other a dumpy little guy with a permanent joyless smile. Always dressed in sports gear, always with an air of menace about them.

"Morning, gentlemen!" said Dav, with his usual fake chumminess. "What can I do you for?"

"What we after, Batman?" said the little one.

"You tell me, Robin," said the big one.

"Something for Bamps, is it?" said Robin.

"Sounds about right," said Batman.

"What you got then, butt?" said Robin.

"Take a look, guys."

The dynamic duo, as Dav liked to call them, progressed down the shop towards Caron. Dav urgently beckoned her into action, but she had no need to approach the pair, as they walked up to her, right up, uncomfortably close.

"Alright love?" said Batman.

Caron backed away a little, preserving her personal space. Batman immediately moved into it. He was viewing her without expression, as if she were part of the furniture.

"What are you looking for?" she asked.

"I think I found it," said Batman, and Robin laughed.

Caron's discomfort grew. Even at her young age, she knew there was something about her which brought out the worst of many men. She was slim and well-proportioned, she walked well, but no-one would have called her beautiful, and for some reason this combination made men want to approach her yet treat her with disrespect. But she would not show she was rattled.

"There's two rows down here," she said. "Take a look and if there's anything you want to know, ask me."

"What's your phone number?" asked Batman.

"Know about the dragons," replied Caron.

"Don't worry, love," said Batman. "We know what we want."

The two men roved down the rows of new cages and stopped at the dragon who had taken such an interest in Caron. Maybe the sharpness of its eye was obvious to them too.

"Does this one flame?" asked Robin.

Caron went into her automatic sales pitch. "We don't guarantee flaming from any of our dragons," she said. "Only steam."

"Bamps wants flame," said Robin.

"Feels the cold, does Bamps," said Batman.

"If you'd like to try our Ruby Street store – " began Caron.

"Tried it, love," interrupted Robin.

"Didn't like it," said Batman.

"It's just that they do guarantee – " began Caron.

"How much is this one?" said Robin.

Caron hesitated. She knew it was her job to sell the dragon, but. . .

"I should point out," she said, "it's got a withered wing."

"So it has," said Robin.

"Not much of a salesman, are you, love?" said Batman.

"Just being honest," said Caron.

Robin raised his eyebrows. Batman gave a snort of laughter. They moved on to the next cage, then the next. A short, hushed conversation, then they decided to buy. There was nothing of note about the dragon they had chosen other than its patchy coat, half brightly coloured, half a dull beige.

What were these guys up to? They'd bought a dragon a week for the past month. They knew full well the dragons were useless as a source of heat.

"We have Firefuel X7 at half price, if you want food for it," said Caron, a line she'd trotted out repeatedly for the past week.

"No thanks love," said Batman. "Bamps has got his own food."

"You know you can't just feed it – "

"We know everything you know, love," said Robin.

"And a lot more," said Batman, with a wink.

Caron took the sale. It would earn her a few quid, money she desperately needed. But what would it mean for that poor pathetic creature? Best not to think about it, she told herself, as the two men carried the caged dragon past a beaming Dav and a less happy Dobbin. That was the third time in a week Dav had given Caron a sales opportunity ahead of him: maybe it was true she was being eyed up for promotion to Ruby

Street. Where was the justice in that, when he'd been at Toad-stool Lane six months longer?

Two

C aron called the dragon Blaze. Unlike Dav and Dobbin, she'd never given a dragon a name before, as she didn't want to get involved with the creatures, even by making jokes about them. But every time she walked down the shop she was drawn to the same cage, as if it was somehow her destiny.

She knew what her friend Rosa would have said. Caron and the dragon had known each other in a past life. Rosa had lots of theories like that, which she talked about with total conviction, but Caron was too hard-headed to believe anything which could not be proved. But there had always been people she'd felt a connection with, often instantly - Elfin, for example - and the sense that whatever drew them together would have existed wherever or whenever they met.

Blaze, however, was not a person. Just the one creature in the shop with curiosity. Curiosity which was feeding Caron's own curiosity, to the point of obsession.

"Caz!"

Dav, as usual, was watching her. Not out of his own curiosity, just anxiety that any of the sellers might have nothing to do.

"Get over the warehouse and check the tags"

Caron steeled herself. The warehouse, as it was called, was where they kept the part-exchange creatures, taken from customers as part payment for dragons. It was actually over the road, through the memorial masons' yard and up a flight of perilous metal steps, as the building was sited over the workshop where the masons made their gravestones. You could hear them chipping way down there, if the creatures weren't moaning or whining, as most were in an even sadder state than the dragons. But what made the warehouse particularly creepy was that it was built in the shape of an L, and you never knew what or who was round the corner. Customers had been known to find their way up there, even though it was supposed to be locked, and to be alone with a strange man, or more than one, was an uncomfortable experience.

Caron checked the tags on the cages and the water tanks. These were tiny security devices, linked to the sellers' phones, to guard against theft. If an animal was sold, the tag was taken off. But there was always the danger someone would spot the tag and remove it themselves, especially in the warehouse where there were no security cameras. So they were regularly checked, a tedious, time-consuming job.

Everything seemed to be in order: no sign any stranger had been in the warehouse unsupervised. Even so, Caron kept a broom handy and held her breath as she turned the corner of the L. But just as she felt relieved to find the space empty, there was a clatter on the metal steps. Someone was coming up.

Caron prepared herself. If it was Dav or Dobbin, no problem. Curtis, the van driver, or the old man, not so good. A stray customer, panic stations.

But it was none of these. Much to Caron's surprise, it was Farah, the window dresser. Or so she was called, though Farah was responsible for every aspect of design in the Dekker empire: window displays, store layouts, business cards, website, even the decoration of the vans. Caron was in awe of her talent but uncomfortable in her presence. So were others, but that was because of her disability, the one thing about her that didn't bother Caron. Caron's uncle had cerebral palsy and used a wheelchair, so the fact Farah walked with one foot turned inward was no big deal to her. What bothered her more were the questions Farah would ask her, the kind of questions a best friend might ask, not someone who barely knew her.

"Oh" said the window dresser. "What are you doing here?"

That in itself was an odd question, as it was surely the question Caron should have been asking, except she didn't need to, as Farah went into a long explanation of how she was updating the website, without waiting for Caron's answer.

Caron listened dutifully, then made a show of adjusting the feeder on a turtle's tank.

"Do you enjoy doing this?" asked Farah.

Caron considered her answer carefully. Farah did not look like a standard employee, with her bony, boyish face and short, swept-back hair, but she was surely close to Jac Dekker, and Caron suspected that anything she told her would get relayed to the boss.

"I like a challenge," she replied.

"So you don't enjoy doing this," Farah shot back.

Caron felt herself blush. But Farah was not finished.

"What do you think of Mr Dekker?" she asked.

Caron's blush deepened. "I don't really know him," she said.

"Don't you think it's amazing, how he built all this up from nothing?"

"Did he? I don't know about that."

"Well you know now"

"Ok"

"So don't you think it's amazing?"

Caron could not bring herself to answer. She was doing her job, wasn't that enough?

"I've got to get back to the shop," she said.

Farah tipped her head to one side and viewed Caron lengthily. "You're very young," she said.

"So?" said Caron. It was a comment she heard often. People still hadn't got used to the fact that the law had changed. Back in the day it was immigrant workers who worked for peanuts, but when they put a stop to that, hey presto, kids could leave school a year earlier to take all the rubbish jobs. Most still lived at home, which cut down their living expenses, but Caron didn't have that luxury.

"It's just an observation," said Farah. "I'm sure you're very capable."

"I am."

Farah continued to view her, much to Caron's discomfort, then suddenly took a new tack. "Did you hear the tide forecast?" she asked.

"Why?"

"It's bad. This place could be flooded next week."

"Yeah?" Caron's guard was up. Why was Farah suddenly talking to her about this? Was this another kind of test?

"People need to take climate change seriously," continued Farah.

Caron said nothing. She was not getting drawn into a conversation about politics.

"This place could be flooded," Farah repeated.

"Let's hope not," replied Caron.

"Yes," said Farah, nodding eagerly. "Let's hope not." She put a hand on Caron's forearm, which Caron swiftly removed.

Three

Caron knew all about the upcoming storm. On the wall of her small flat was a map of the town with the areas likely to be flooded marked in different colours, according to how high the sea might rise. Toadstool Lane was a goner even with a relatively small rise, while Ruby Street and her flat, being situated up the hill, were safe unless the rise was astronomical – not that Caron counted that out. Caron distrusted all official pronouncements about the subject, not because she didn't believe in man-made climate change – far from it – but why trust the TV services owned by billionaires who profited from airlines or major construction projects?

Caron studied the map for at least the hundredth time - yes, she knew she was obsessive, but unlike so many others, she understood the dangers of water. It had been her job at home to empty the garden waste bin, and from an early age had had the determination to lift the thing, even when full of grass and cuttings. But when the lid had been left off, and rain had half-filled it, she could not move it an inch. Yes, water was unbelievably heavy, and it was no surprise to her that a mass of it could uproot trees and destroy buildings. You messed with it at your peril.

Enough of that. Caron's eyes strayed to the new photo beside the map. What *was* it about that dragon? Could it somehow understand something about her, something she didn't understand herself? The thought was exciting to her, but at the same time a seed of anxiety was growing. Life was only possible for Caron at Toadstool Lane if it was a half-life. Relationships of any kind threatened to derail her.

Yes, it was better to keep her distance from that little creature.

But if the flood warnings were right. . .

Caron mentally replayed her conversation with Farah. No, she wasn't being paranoid, the window dresser was testing her out, no question. Checking what she thought of Jak Dekker, moving onto the environmental threat. . .should Caron have pretended she didn't care about the latter, and thought the world of the former? She could hear her dad's voice scoffing. For God's sake, what was wrong with her? Why couldn't she be like her sister Elsie, keeping in with the right people, doing and saying whatever would bring her success? Yes, look at Elsie, a real chip off the old block, now practically running his roofing business!

Pity she was also a narrow-minded bigot who believed everything she heard on Patriot News.

"I might have to kill you one day," Elsie had told her, last time they'd met.

Caron shut off all thoughts of her family, put on a dance track and focussed on tidying her little flat, a thankless task as it was sure to be as much of a mess in a day's time. But her labours were soon interrupted by a phone call – possibly the phone call she had least expected, given her conversation with Farah.

It was Dav. In a sombre voice, he told her she would not be required at Toadstool Lane next morning. Then, hearing her nervous reply, he jovially informed her she would be working at Ruby Street instead.

"Seriously?" she asked.

"Max WIlliams is off," replied Dav, "and for some unaccountable reason, you are first reserve, my girl."

"I can't believe it," said Caron.

"No-one can believe it," said Dav.

Caron did not sleep well that night. Nervous, of course, but exultant too. After all she'd been through, any kind of triumph was desperately welcome. She was no money grabber, but for all her misgivings about the Dekker empire, she was not going to throw up such a golden ticket. Even if it meant dressing like the other women at Ruby Street, conservative and reassuring in their dress suits and court shoes.

Caron removed her so-called Sunday best from their poly covers and put them on. How Caron hated those clothes. And how her mum loved them. "That's my daughter," she'd said, while Caron had thought precisely the opposite. Why did her mum so insist she loved Caron when she disliked the jeans she wore, the music she listened to and the people she hung around with?

She just looked wrong. Yes, the suit fitted her as well as any model, but the face was never meant for it. You couldn't put a witch on a catwalk. Maybe it was a compliment that they'd called her that at school? Yes, her chin was angular and her nose was hooked, but her eyes were as fierce and bright as a polecat's. Rosa said she belonged to an earlier time, a time before technology and home comforts had dulled the senses.

Was that what Blaze had recognised? Were they communicating at a level of instinct that most of the world had lost? It was a question which had peppered Caron's feverish night. But now she had to silence her obsession. She would not be seeing the little dragon, and it would not do to worry that it was missing her.

Caron took down the photo of Blaze and put it in the bedside drawer. Then she texted her mum. Yes, the mum who didn't understand her, who still tolerated the man who'd bullied her. The mum who would inevitably broadcast the news about Ruby Street to friends, family and total strangers, then hassle her endlessly for photos.

But no matter. The morning was fresh, and Caron felt full of hope as she walked the half mile uphill to Ruby Street. She loved this time of day, when few people were about, the delivery trucks were doing their morning rounds and only the all-night café was open. And what a feeling it gave her to stand before the window of the dragon superstore! This was Farah's latest creation, like the set of a fantasy movie, with a huge shimmering dragon wandering about in a landscape of volcanoes under an unearthly opal light. For some reason the word *iri-*

descent came to Caron's mind. It was a word she remembered from the only teacher she had ever listened to, Mr Cummins. Mr Cummins was different to the others. He actually liked it when she wore a skirt which looked different colours from different angles.

Mr Pritchard wouldn't have liked that skirt. Mr Pritchard was the manager of the Ruby Street store, and Caron's first task that morning was to be 'prepared' by him. He was an odd-looking man, short and stout, dressed in a three-piece suit and bow tie, his heavily bespectacled face topped off by a pile of white candy floss hair. Dav had always found it hilarious that his first name was Waylon and he had once done a hoe-down at a staff social, but there was nothing light-hearted about him as he addressed Caron.

"You may have sold dragons at Toadstool Lane," he began, "but don't think you know anything about selling dragons here."

Caron nodded dutifully. She hated him already.

"Customers here expect the very best service. And that is what we expect you to give them."

Again Caron indicated that she understood.

"But it's no great achievement to sell a dragon here. They virtually sell themselves. What matters most are the sundries."

Sundries? That Caron did not understand.

"By sundries I mean first and foremost the breath converters. You get some clever charlies who think they can buy them cheaper on the internet. The first thing they need to know is that using a dragon with a converter we don't supply invalidates the guarantee."

Caron was beginning to feel overwhelmed. Was he deliberately using language she didn't understand?

"I don't know about the guarantee" she said.

Mr Pritchard sat back in his chair in mock surprise. "You don't know about the sales contract?" he asked.

"I've never worked here."

"But don't you have a contract at Toadstool Lane?"

Caron was now close to panic. She began to bluff. "Dav handles all that," she said.

Mr Pritchard's eyes opened wide. "Are you referring to Mr Montague?" he asked.

"Yes, Mr Montague," said Caron, quickly.

Mr Pritchard reached into a nearby filing cabinet and placed an A4 document before Caron. "You'd better make yourself familiar with this before you go anywhere near the sales floor," he said. "All our dragons are guaranteed for ten years. But only if they are sold with our breath converters, and only if they are serviced by our heating engineers every six months. That's where the real profits lie."

Caron picked up the contract and pretended to read, but her head was shot and the words were a meaningless jumble.

"I'll give you ten minutes to absorb that," said Mr Pritchard, "then you can go up to area 2B."

Four

Caron switched off notifications. The last thing she needed was her phone beeping every five minutes. She'd sent her mum a picture of her outfit, the shop window and the packed lunch in her individual pigeonhole – now her mum would have to wait for more. And no, Caron was not replying to the text asking if there were any nice young men working in the store. But there certainly were a lot of people working there, far more than she'd imagined. The company offices were right next to area 2B, where the stock clerk, the finance officer and numerous secretaries worked – then there were the cleaners, the drivers and van boys, not to mention one salesperson for every area.

No two areas were the same. Each featured one monster dragon in a setting designed to emphasise its particular qualities: a primeval gravel pit, a make-believe lake, a cactus-studded oasis. The only common feature were the slogans, printed or projected: ENERGY FOR LIFE, BREATH OF LIFE, DREAM GREEN TODAY.

Caron's dragon was a salmon pink monster with a shimmering turquoise crest on its head. It would certainly have made a great showpiece in the foyer of an expensive hotel or holiday mansion. But when it turned its eyes towards her it made her shiver. They were chillingly cold, like the lights of a machine. It was so unnerving, with no customers about, just her and this great alien presence, and no knowing what was on its mind.

Thankfully someone did eventually come along. He was a dapper little man in a pale grey suit, about thirty. In his hand was a cage.

"Hello, love," he said. "I'm Jason."

"I'm Caron," replied Caron, relieved to be on first name terms with anybody.

"Brunch time," said Jason.

"Oh," said Caron. "I didn't know we had a break."

Jason gave out a short, high-pitched laugh. "Not for you, love!" he said. He opened an aperture in the dragon's enclosure, pressed the cage against it and released what was inside. Caron immediately recognised a rock cavy, basically a genetically modified guinea pig about the size of a chicken. The rock cavy hobbled forward a few steps, sniffing, at which point it caught the eye of the dragon, which turned smartly to face it and immediately sent out a rose-tinged blue flame like an almighty blowtorch. The rock cavy was instantly cremated, whereupon the dragon lumbered forward, seized the remains in its jaws and swallowed it in two gulping mouthfuls.

Caron could not hide her disgust.

"You'll get used to it, love," said Jason.

"Can't it just eat pellets?" asked Caron.

"We get better quality waste this way," replied Jason. He went on to explain the operation in the basement, where the dragon waste arrived down chutes to be processed into building materials by the Temps. The Temps were immigrants, so did not officially exist. They had no rights whatsoever and could be swiftly exported the moment they lost their jobs.

"Sounds awful," said Caron.

"Best not to think about it," said Jason. "Well, Caron, I must love you and leave you. Have a nice day."

"Nice to meet you," said Caron.

"Shame about Mr Williams," said Jason.

Caron was baffled. Why was it a shame, if Mr Williams was just off for the day? But before she could ask for more explanation, Jason was gone, and her mind had to swiftly switch focus: two customers had wandered in. A middle-aged couple, he in pale blue shirt and beige trousers, the age-old costume of the rich, she in a dark blue dress suit with white lace trim. They were obviously happy with what they had found.

"Oo, I like this one," said the woman.

"Claws like grappling hooks," said the man.

"They do say it's a good sign."

Caron made herself known. "Can I help at all?" she asked. Instinctively she'd adopted a posher accent than was normal to her.

"Do you know its age?" asked the woman, unexpectedly.

"I'm not absolutely sure about that," replied Caron, "but it is in premium condition."

"Oh, we know that," said the man. "Mr Dekker wouldn't sell any rubbish."

"We're personal friends of Mr Dekker," added the woman.

It was a familiar refrain. Half the customers at Toadstool Lane claimed to be personal friends of Mr Dekker.

Caron pressed on with the patter she'd been preparing for the past hour. She was aware she was talking too quickly and maybe too intensely, but she had to grudgingly admit that Mr Pritchard had been right: the dragon was selling itself. The couple clearly wanted it.

Now for the sundries.

"We do recommend this converter for use with this dragon," she said, indicating the Sasaki Respire on display.

"No thank you," said the man. "We'll be getting a converter on the internet."

"We really wouldn't recommend that," said Caron, hastily. "You may only get a fraction of the performance from some of these converters."

"Even if they're a Sasaki Respire?" said the man.

"They may call them that," said Caron, bluffing madly, "but the market's flooded with fakes. If you buy here you know you've got a genuine model."

The man did not look convinced.

"That's why we only guarantee our dragons if used with our converters," continued Caron. Her face felt hot: she was hopelessly out of her depth.

"Perhaps we ought to think about it," said the woman.

"Such a shame," said the man,

"You must buy it!" blurted Caron, and instantly regretted it. She'd become an embarrassment, a stupid little girl in women's clothes, all the things her dad had called her.

At this point a fourth voice rang out across the sales floor. "Mr and Mrs Curtis!"

All eyes turned to the rotund little man scurrying towards them: none other than Jac Dekker, on his rubbery face a broad smile. He shook hands warmly with his two customers who were clearly delighted to see him.

"How are you two?" he asked.

"Very well thank you, Mr Dekker," they replied in unison.

"And how is Betsi?" asked Mr Dekker. "Did she get into St Hilda's?"

"She did," said the man.

"Oh, very well done!" said Mr Dekker. "You must be so delighted."

"Relieved," said the woman.

"Well, yes. Those personal tutors were very expensive."

"Too expensive," said the man.

"Oh, come on now, Rhys," said the woman.

"Now, have you come to buy one of my dragons?" asked Mr Dekker.

"Possibly," said the man.

"And has Miss Bell been looking after you?" asked Mr Dekker.

"Well, yes, she's explained everything," said the man, much to Caron's relief.

"Well, come on now, you must have this dragon!"

"We like it very much," said the woman. "It's just that. . ."

"Yes?"

"We wanted to get a converter on the internet, but Miss Bell tells us the dragon will not be guaranteed if we do that."

"But Mrs Curtis, you don't know what you're buying on the internet! Always buy from someone you trust! Don't you trust me?"

"Of course we do, Mr Dekker. But it's the same model."

Mr Dekker drew a deep breath. "Now look," he says. "As we're friends, I'm going to offer you a deal. But this is strictly between you and me, you understand? Whatever you are paying on the internet, you'll pay the same price here."

"That's very generous of you, Mr Dekker."

"My pleasure. But it's our little secret. If everyone else hears of this, they'll all want the same deal, and I'll be out of business!"

"Our lips are sealed, Mr Dekker. Thank you so much." Mrs Curtis gave a trill of delight and hugged her husband.

"Sort out the paperwork, will you, Miss Bell?" said Mr Dekker, directly addressing Caron for the first time, without the warm smile he clearly reserved for his friends.

Five

Caron's finger tapped manically on her calculator, her excitement growing. Her name was on the sales documents which meant the commission on the sale was hers. "Commission" was a new word to her when she joined Dekkers, but now she well understood what it meant: five per cent of the takings. So, dragon. . .converter. . .unbelievable! She'd earnt in one morning more than she earnt in a week at Toadstool Lane!

And even better, more than her beloved father earnt in a day!

So, just enough time to send Mum a text and photo, while the sold dragon was dosed with Somnadine and removed, and the replacement brought in: another impressive beast, similar to the first one, but the tables were turned now. The dragon was the newcomer, unsure of its territory, whereas Caron was feeling increasingly at home. She had her patter all prepared, and would not be thrown if another customer mentioned the internet.

As it happened, the next customer was not a customer at all. A frail-looking old woman wandered into the area, wearing a blue-and-white gingham dustcoat: at first Caron thought she might be a cleaner on her lunch break, till she noticed the woman was also wearing what appeared to be slippers. Her hair was unnaturally black, clearly dyed, her face wore a benign smile, and her head shook slightly, as if she had a nervous condition or maybe the early stages of Parkinsons.

"Hello, love," she said, and it was immediately clear to Caron that she was not there to buy a dragon.

"Hello," said Caron.

"Nice and warm in here."

"The dragon likes it warm."

"Oh, it is marvellous."

Caron was dimly aware that she ought to be ushering the old woman out of the shop, but she felt strangely comfortable having her there. It did not bother Caron one bit that the woman was eccentric: Caron had always felt at home around eccentrics. And after all, she was doing no harm: why shouldn't she look at the dragon?

"I'll just have a sweet, if it's all the same to you," said the woman.

"Suit yourself," said Caron.

The woman fished into her bag, unwrapped a toffee and began sucking it with expressions of delight. "Would you like one?" she asked.

"Ok," said Caron.

The woman gave Caron a toffee, and the two of them stood quietly chewing, observed with vague interest by the cold-eyed dragon.

"I think he wants one," said the woman.

"Probably."

"I'm Jean, by the way."

"Hi Jean. I'm Caron."

"I've not seen you here before."

"No, first day."

"Oh, really? Holiday job, is it?"

Caron wondered exactly what holiday Jean was referring to but thought it best not to ask. They carried on chewing softly, in silence.

"You remind me of my girl," said the woman, eventually.

"Yeah? Does she live round here?"

The woman gave a soft, sad laugh. "Life goes on," she said. "We have to make the best of it, don't we?"

At this point Mr Pritchard burst into the space, puffing and blowing, closely followed by Bryn, the company handyman, and according to Dav, Mr Dekker's personal enforcer.

"Out!" commanded Mr Pritchard.

Caron was dumbstruck. Was Mr Pritchard really speaking like that to Jean? For heaven's sake, she wasn't a shoplifter or a hooligan!

"I'm just having a look," said Jean, as if she could read Caron's mind.

"We're not a zoo," said Mr Pritchard. He and Bryn now stood either side of her, like prison guards. "Come on, out!"

For all Caron's doubts and fears, she was an instinctively brave person, the first person to step in when someone was being picked on or in danger. Every fibre of her being was telling her to defend Jean, but she knew the price she would pay for this. So she stood as impotent as a doll as Jean was more-or-less frogmarched from the building.

Mr Pritchard then returned to the area, still puffed up by his show of authority. "If she comes in again, give me a call straight away," he said.

"She wasn't doing any harm," said Caron.

Mr Pritchard took this for what it was, a challenge. "Listen, Miss Bell," he said. "You are not employed to pass the time of day with any good-for-nothing who wanders in. You are employed to sell dragons. This is a top-of-the-range store, not a public convenience."

Caron was livid. How could he describe Jean as good for nothing? He knew nothing about her. As far as Caron was concerned, she was good for a lot more than the pompous oaf now facing her.

"We can't just throw someone out because they haven't bought something," she said.

"I'm sorry?" rasped Mr Pritchard. "Are you now the manager? Are you telling me who we can allow in this shop? Because for your information, this store is private property, and we are fully entitled to ban anybody we choose. And if you want to progress here, you had better not question that."

"I'm only here for the day."

"Are you?"

"Well, yes."

"That's not what I've been told."

Jason's earlier comment came back to Caron. "Isn't Mr Williams back tomorrow?" she asked.

Mr Pritchard was not about to give a straight answer. "I believe Mr Dekker will be having words with you later," he said.

Six |

Caron climbed out of the taxi and surveyed the two massive gates before her. She had seen gates like this in films, usually horror films, but had never imagined herself the other side of them. But truth was proving stranger than fiction, and for whatever reason she had been invited to the house of Jac Dekker, deep in the wealthiest suburb of Llantresedd.

Caron shivered. Night was falling and she had not anticipated how suddenly the temperature would drop. She wore her work clothes and a thin jacket, no hat, no scarf, no gloves. Still, she could surely be confident that Jac Dekker's mansion would be as warm as a top-of-the-range dragon could make it.

Some kind of intercom was attached to the gatepost. It looked fiendishly complicated. But just as Caron was puzzling how to use it, the gates began oh-so-slowly to open: a car was about to exit the driveway. Seizing the opportunity, Caron ducked inside the gates just as a Mercedes Phi eased out onto the road.

Caron was now faced with a long, dimly-lit drive leading to a gigantic house, which looked vaguely like a select private hospital. She set off with her usual confident rangey walk, but that was not how she was feeling inside. Why was it necessary to have such a long drive? Her nerves were turning to irritation.

The house proved to be well defended. A deep waterless moat ran round the outside, so that the only part that could be accessed was the front door. Surprisingly, there were no curtains or blinds visible at the windows, so Caron could see through to the space-age kitchen, metallic and spotless, with video screens and what appeared to be four or five ovens. A woman about the same size, shape and age as Jac Dekker was in there, but as it was now dark outside, there would be no way she could see Caron.

Caron approached the front door. Through the textured glass she could see another door quite close: clearly a small entrance hall or porch. So where was the doorbell?

There was no doorbell. No doorbell, no knocker, no intercom.

Caron began to realise she may have made a mistake not using the intercom at the gate.

A gust of chill wind brought out the goosebumps on Caron's hand as she rapped on the hard glass.

No reply.

Caron rapped harder, fearing (rightly) that the porch was acting as a soundproof barrier.

Still no reply.

Now Caron went into full-scale stress. She had been so careful not to arrive late, and now she was imagining Jac Dekker checking his Rolex and frowning. She began to hammer with both fists and shout, but it was as futile as screaming in space. And why oh why hadn't she worn a warmer coat? It was so cold and getting colder by the second.

What options did she have? She had her phone, but not Jac Dekker's number, stupid girl! She could go back to the gate, but the gate would be locked, no possible way over it. God, what if she was trapped there all night? She would surely freeze to death! Be found like a dead rabbit, make the local news headlines, confirm her mother's worst fears, justify everything her father had ever said!

Someone had to hear her! She raced round to face the big kitchen window, waving her arms frantically, crying "Hello!" at the top of her lungs. Mrs Dekker, if that's who she was, continued to potter about inside, completely oblivious. A young man came in, exchanged a few words, left with a cake.

Back to the front door, hammering again, tears now brimming. Shoe off, hammering with that, heel breaking off, not even a mark on the solid glass panels. Tears streaming: her best court shoes, the ones Mum loved, ruined.

Dav would have his number. Dav could text him. But at what cost? She would be exposed as an idiot, her worst fear, and Dav would never let her hear the end of it.

She rang Dav. She did her level best to sound calm, offhand even, but she could not hide the tremor in her voice. He actually asked if she was OK, which brought an involuntary sob out of her, destroying any pretence that she was. But he agreed to text the old man, and with a stream of apologies, she ended the call.

A minute later, the door opened, and Dekker peered out.

"Hello?" he said.

Caron burst past him into the house, gabbling frantically, hardly aware of what she was saying. Why was there no doorbell? Everyone has a doorbell! She had been on time, well on time, it wasn't her fault she had been stuck in the freezing cold for twenty minutes!

Dekker, needless to say, was not expecting this barrage. But if he was flummoxed, he did not show it.

"What happened to your shoe?" he asked.

Caron felt a sob rising but fought it. *Control yourself*, a voice inside her cried. *You sound like a mad witch.*

"Sorry," she said. "Can I get a hot drink?"

"Tea? Coffee?"

Caron drank neither but feared making herself sound even more weird. "Tea, thanks," she said.

"Milk? Sugar?"

It seemed a bafflingly hard question. "Er. . .everything, please."

"If you'd like to go through."

Dekker indicated the doors to some kind of lounge, and for the first time Caron became aware of where she was standing, in a large lobby more like the reception area of a hotel: half way up the wall ahead of them was a huge tank occupied by the most sensational dragon she had ever seen: almost twice the size of the beast she'd sold that day, a riot of colour and muscular beauty. And yet. . .

. . .no, she had to put Blaze out of her mind.

Caron entered the lounge. Like everything else in the house, it was enormous, more like the departure lounge of a small airport. Not one, not two, but three white leather sofas, modern, angular, to her mind unwelcoming. But then nothing was that welcoming in the room: glass-and-chrome tables, great showy mirrors, monster chandeliers. . .how could anyone feel at home there? Only a man who felt comforted by wealth.

"Please, please sit down, Miss Bell," said Dekker in the same genial, hustling manner he employed with his customers.

Caron sat on the edge of the nearest sofa, feeling anything but relaxed. The woman she presumed to be Mrs Dekker came in with a cup of tea and a plate of fancy cakes, which she placed on an occasional table next to Caron before explaining in great detail what they all were, blithely unaware that Caron was unable to take in a single word.

As soon as Mrs Dekker had left, Jac Dekker pulled up a chair opposite Caron, who immediately diverted her eyes, taking a sudden interest in a marble vase on a nearby shelf.

"You like my ornament?" asked Dekker.

"Yes," said Caron, hastily.

"I do appreciate a nice ornament," said Dekker.

Caron chanced a glance in his direction, only to witness a great toothy smile which made her shiver. Was he referring to her? She tugged her skirt self-consciously over her knees.

"So," said Dekker. "Where do you see yourself in twenty years' time?"

It was a question Caron was utterly unprepared for. God, she didn't know where she'd be next week, let alone twenty years! Dead? Homeless? Living in a commune in Casablanca?

"Um. . .a teacher maybe?" she replied.

It was not an answer which pleased Dekker.

"Oh," he said. "So you don't intend to pursue a career in sales?"

"I don't know," said Caron. "Maybe."

"I think you should."

"Do you?"

"Why do you think I've invited you here?"

"I don't know."

"You're surely aware that there's a vacancy?"

"Not really."

"Well why do you think you were working in the shop to-day?"

"Because Mr Williams was off."

Dekker's face suddenly became serious. "Mr Williams won't be coming back," he said.

"Oh," said Caron. "Why's that?"

"His doctor's note was not satisfactory."

"Why not?"

"I don't accept depression as a reason for missing work."

Caron could not disguise her reaction to this statement. She knew the full meaning of the word *depression*. But Dekker clearly didn't.

"Can you imagine," he continued, "running a shop where the sellers take a day off every time they feel down in the dumps?

"It's not – "

"We'd be out of business in a month, Miss Bell. And then no-one would have a job."

"But – "

"I get down in the dumps. My wife gets down in the dumps. But we don't sit around feeling sorry for ourselves. That's why we're living in a house like this. Wouldn't you like to live in a house like this?"

Again Caron could not disguise her feelings. The memory of Jean came back to her, her encounters with Mr Pritchard, the nightmare half hour stuck on the Dekkers' driveway. How much more would she have to swallow to get the big pay-cheque?

"Not really" she said.

"No?"

"I prefer smaller houses."

"You do?"

"Where you have neighbours."

Even as she said these things, Caron could hear her mother screaming in her ear. *What the hell are you doing, Caron? Are you mad?*

"Well," said Dekker. "You are a disappointment to me, Miss Bell."

"Sorry."

"I was about to offer you a three-month trial period at Ruby Street."

"Sorry."

"When I was your age I'd have cut off my right arm for a chance like that."

"Then you were lucky you weren't, weren't you?"

It was the kind of quip Caron had made many times in her life, and she inwardly winced as if expecting her father's heavy hand in return. But Dekker, more disturbingly, smiled.

Five minutes later a taxi pulled up in front of the house. Miss Bell's job interview was over.

Seven

So there would be no tenfold increase in pay, nor a luxury crib to show her dad. Yet Caron felt strangely relaxed as she returned to Toadstool Lane next morning. It was so natural to her to be honest, sometimes too honest people would say, and it was as if a little steam had escaped from the boiling kettle that was her head. She really should have known that she would never have fitted in at Ruby Street, but sometimes you had to go through things to be sure. Why oh why, however, had she still felt she had to please her mum? She really wished she hadn't told her. That was the real downer, having to deal with endless friends and relatives asking how she got on.

Dav already knew of course. That was obvious by the look of delight on his face. A reception committee was gathered around him: Dobbin, Farah, Curtis the van driver and Cai the van boy. A big cheer went up as Caron walked in.

"Miss Bell!" cried Dav. "What *have* you done?"

"Nothing much," said Caron, attempting to move past.

"Wo, wo," said Dav, blocking her way.. "We want the whole story, Caz! How the hell did you get an invite to the old man's house. . .and end up with an amber warning?!"

"What?" said Caron. She could not hide her alarm. Dekker had given her an amber warning? It was the first she knew about it.

"Did you take a dump in his dragon tank?"

General laughter, none louder than Dobbin's.

"How do you know I've got an amber warning?" said Caron.

"How do you think? I'm the manager! I'm in charge of what is laughingly called discipline in this store!"

Caron was devastated. She knew she'd blown any chance of working at Ruby Street, but it had never occurred to her she might be sacked from Toadstool Lane. And for what? For saying she liked small houses?

"You'd better knuckle down, Caz," said Dav, in a more serious voice.

"What, or you'll report me?" muttered Caron.

"If I have to, yes," said Dav. "Because if I don't, it'll be my job on the line."

"Thanks."

"You or me, Caz."

He meant it.

"I'm going to the toilet," said Caron.

"I thought I could smell something," quipped Dobbin.

"Don't give up the day job," snapped Caron. She hurried from the sales floor and through the tearoom door, mind in turmoil. Ok, she hadn't said what Jak Dekker wanted to hear, but he'd shown no sign of even being mildly upset! To give her an amber warning. . .well, she knew he was ruthless but could never have imagined what it felt like to be the victim of it. The next step was red, and the step after that. . .it didn't bear thinking about. She was as trapped as if she were in a cage.

The thought of Blaze only increased her anxiety. She had to get back on an even keel and any kind of emotional involvement would get in the way of that. She had to be hard. She had to get on with her work like a robot.

"Ah, Caron!" trilled Dav, seeing her reappear. "I have a nice job for you. The end cages need sanitising. The good news is, there's one less to do."

"You've sold one?"

"Sure have. One up to the Dobmeister."

"And a converter," added Dobbin, smugly.

Caron steeled herself and walked down the shop with a composed air. If Blaze was gone, she reasoned, it was all for the best. Yet her hands were shaking.

But the cage was still there, as was the little dragon, though rolled into a ball with its face turned away. Caron could not deny the wave of relief that swept over her. So much for being a robot.

"Blaze?" she said, quietly.

The dragon's head swivelled round and its eyes opened wide. Yes, it had remembered her! But before she could engage with it, Dav and Dobbin were on the scene.

"Don't worry," said Dav. "We've still got the wingless wonder."

"I wasn't worried," said Caron.

"Dobbin's taught it a trick, haven't you, Dobs?"

Dobbin produced a thin white bar: an eggstick, sometimes used as a treat for the dragons. "Watch this," he said, poking the stick towards the bars of the cage.

Blaze did not respond.

"Damn!" said Dobbin. "It's not doing it!"

"What's supposed to happen?" asked Caron.

"I'd trained it to shake its butt," said Dobbin.

"Why?" said Caron.

"Cos it was funny!" said Dobbin. "Come on, you little – "

Blaze turned its head back to the rear of the cage.

"It's trying to make you look stupid, Dobs," said Dav. "Not that that's difficult."

"Stupid thing," said Dobbin.

Dav and Dobbin departed, and as if sensing the coast was clear, Blaze turned back towards Caron. Possibly it needed to clear its eye, but Caron liked to think it gave her a wink.

"You're not stupid, are you?" she said. "Neither of us are."

For a moment Caron was back in Year 10, getting her report from Mr Cummins. Mr Cummins had described her as *highly intelligent*. Not just hardworking, not just able, *highly intelligent*. It had embarrassed her. She wondered if he had said it just because he liked her a lot. But despite her brittle confidence, there was a little voice inside her which told her it might be true.

Nothing seemed to settle Caron's mind now. No matter how hard she tried to return to her old routines, the day in Ruby Street haunted her, and when Batman and Robin appeared, her usual sinking feeling was replaced by unashamed loathing. What an obnoxious pair of strutting pigeons they were, a puffed-up duo of overgrown school bullies out for nothing but their own glory. How she would have loved to take them down. But she was on a yellow warning, and it was her job to serve them.

"Looking for another dragon?" she asked.

"That's why we're here," said Robin.

"What happened to the last one?" she asked, risking a little informality.

"Bamps didn't like it," said Robin.

"Wrong colour," said Batman.

"Sold it on," said Robin.

"You could have brought it back for part-exchange," said Caron.

The two men looked at each other and laughed.

"Nah," said Batman. "I don't think so."

Caron briefly considered asking what was so funny but thought the better of it. Instead she went onto autopilot, the standard patter, stressing the winning qualities of each of the dragons, apart from the hopeless one with the withered wing. As before, the dynamic duo were little influenced by what she had to say: they knew what they were looking for, and chose a dragon virtually identical to the one which was apparently the wrong colour. Caron did not even bother to try to sell a converter or food, and prepared the sales documents as they wandered off to have a fake-matey chat with Dav.

As per the usual routine, Caron prepared to remove the tracking tag from its hiding place on the back of the cage. Then she paused.

Would anyone notice if she left it on?

Eight

At first the tracker showed nothing remarkable. The cage had arrived at Heol Y Felin, a road on the new estate built on the site of the old paper mill. Some people said it was idiocy to build a new estate at sea level, with the sea rising year on year, but it didn't seem to deter people from spending a fortune to live there, especially with the new super school nearby. It did seem an odd place for an old person to move to, however, if, indeed, Batman's so-called Bamps really existed. And you might have expected people who lived there to be shopping on Ruby Street, not Toadstool Lane.

Just after dark, however, the cage was on the move again. It was heading out of town, along the coast road.

Caron put on a coat – a warm one this time – stuffed a scarf into the pocket and reached for her crash helmet. She had not ridden her vehicle – an old pizza delivery scooter - since crashing into a ditch two months before and had seriously wondered if she would ever risk it again. But it was her only way of following the dynamic duo, and that she was determined to do, regardless of the dangers.

The coast road was an eerie place at night: nothing but high, dense fir trees on one side, nothing but marshland to the other, from which arose a robotic clanking. This, Caron realised, was the sound of piledrivers hammering down defences against the rising seawater. She'd read an article in the local media about it: the family firm of a local politician had got the contract. The article had made Caron angry, other people as well, but nothing seemed to have changed because of it.

No time to think about that now. Caron had other concerns. It might have helped Caron's state of mind to know where she was going, but the tracking signal just kept moving, apparently towards the middle of nowhere.

Caron's head went back to a happier time: summer, going down that same road in the family car. Her dad in a good mood, stopping at a service station then showering Caron and Elsie with bars of chocolate. Even then the girls bickered, but that deep divide was not there: in many ways they were alike. Even put on little shows together. Back then Elsie never said she might have to kill Caron one day.

Back to reality. The signal had stopped. Caron's phone-map indicated this was at the Skylarks Holiday Park, but it clearly needed updating. Skylarks, where Caron had stayed more than once, had closed over ten years before. As far as Caron was aware, there was nothing there now.

But Caron was wrong. As soon as she approached the site it was clear that most of the buildings remained, though in a predictably sorry state. The great welcoming entrance sign which had once so excited Caron lay flat on the ground, edges rotted, the reception was boarded up, the nearby climbing frame half lost in brambles and nettles. In the distance the happy holiday chalets were looming shadows; it was just possible to make out the higher rooves of the entertainment centre and swimming pool.

Two vans were parked on the old car park; other than those there were no signs of life. A pair of vending machines had been pushed over onto their sides next to reception, as if to form a makeshift barrier; otherwise there seemed to be nothing to stop Caron exploring the area. But just as she climbed off her bike, headlights appeared behind her, and she hastily hid up behind the last remaining bin in what used to be the waste disposal area.

A car pulled into the car park. Four men got out and immediately set off past reception in a way that suggested they were familiar with the place. But before Caron could follow, more cars and vans began to arrive: even a minibus. The visitors were overwhelmingly male, of various ages: just a few women, and none that Caron felt inclined to get to know, not that that was an option. But there was safety in numbers, and as soon as Caron felt it was safe to do so, she slipped out of her hiding place and joined the growing throng. Under the night sky, lit by just a few torches, the procession seemed almost biblical. But Caron had a strong sense these people were not seeking spiritual salvation.

They passed the chalets where Caron had once stayed: broken windows, signs of fire, random furniture strewn over the verandahs. They passed the toilets where Caron had once been potty-trained, the launderette where Elsie had lost her new t-shirt, the café where Caron's dad had once had a frightening row with a man who commented on his trainers. Up ahead was the remains of the indoor pool, a place of intense excitement to the young Caron – always so frenetically noisy, the water warm, the slide terrifying: was there ever a greater experience?

Lo and behold, that building was the crowd's destination. Despite being in no better state of repair than the rest of the site, there were flashing lights inside, and pounding music.

An illegal rave? Surely they had died out decades ago! And these people – they just didn't seem the type.

Caron pulled up the collar of her coat. Even amongst this crowd she was sure she would stick out like a sore thumb. Once inside that place she would no longer have the advantage of dim light, and if Batman and Robin were in there, they would surely recognise her.

It wasn't too late to beat a retreat. But Caron could not bring herself to do it. She was drawn to the doors of the indoor pool just as magnetically as she had been as a child. Remembering the scarf in her pocket, she covered the lower half of her face and followed the procession into the building.

Even in her lowest moments Caron could not have imagined such a gruesome transformation. The waterless pool and the great white girders holding up the roof were covered in graffiti, the lockers around the walls smashed, the once smooth turquoise flooring covered in filth. No laughter, no childish shrieks of excitement, just a mass of virtually silent adults, as if in some kind of purgatory, eyes turned to three figures controlling the sound system where Caron's beloved slide once stood.

The old stone steps leading down into the corner of the pool were still there, but for some reason no-one had ventured down. The crowd remained packed around the fringes, almost as if the pool was still full of water, or was taboo, like going to the altar in a church.

Suddenly a voice boomed out over the PA: *Get ready, my friends – the show's about to start.*

Immediately a new energy, almost frenetic, erupted. And oh God, there they were - Batman and Robin, moving through the crowd, hustling feverishly. Whatever they were selling, they were selling in spades: there was barely a second between one credit card and the next. Meanwhile another pair of entrepreneurs were working the crowd on the other side, close to Caron. She nervously felt for the card wallet in her bag.

For a moment one of the sellers made eye contact. He had a flattened nose. Boxer, thought Caron. Was he part of the entertainment? Whatever, he had little interest in her. On to the next customer.

Ok, my friends. The time has come. . .

Five. . .

The crowd, which had been so silent, joined in a deafening countdown. The lights which had been focussed on the sound system now turned onto the empty pool. Down the steps into this space came two more pairs of men, each pair carrying a hessian sack. They set these sacks a metre apart, untied the drawstrings which held them closed, and backed swiftly away.

To a great guttural roar from the crowd, two dazed creatures emerged: the two second quality dragons Caron had sold that week. Their wings were clipped and the distress in their eyes told Caron that they were desperately hungry. This was a state, as all dragon sellers knew, which completely changed their characters.

There was no question as to what would happen next. Caron covered her eyes but could not escape the horrific shriek that told her that teeth, or claws, had hit their mark. Another shriek followed, but after that it was impossible to hear anything above the savage yells of the crowd. Despite herself Caron felt impelled to uncover her eyes, just in time to see one of the dragons make a doomed effort to fly, only to find itself seized by the neck in the second dragon's jaws.

There would clearly be no mercy. This was a fight to the death.

Caron could face no more. She fought her way through the crowd and out of the building. Then she was violently sick.

Nine

Caron was too young to remember when dragons were first created, but her mum had told her all about it. The government had given billions to Portentum, the company whose experiments in genetic engineering promised to create the new species. Many people had been opposed to this, some of them violently, but they had been outnumbered by those who had been convinced by government propaganda: that these heat-producing creations would provide a source of cheap sustainable energy, so that we would see no more pensioners dying of hypothermia or children too frozen to do their homework.

But people had clearly been duped. Pensioners were still dying. Children were still miserably cold. All those with second quality homes, eating second quality food, could only afford second quality dragons, and no-one knew better than Caron how inadequate these were. So it should have come as no surprise that creatures so denigrated and despised should have become objects of sadistic sport.

That did not mean that Caron was about to accept it. That same instinct that made her the first person to step in when someone was bullied, now fuelled her marching feet towards

Toadstool Lane that next morning. The whole world was going to know about the obscene events she had witnessed, and one way or another, she was going to put an stop to them.

"Dav!" she yelled, the moment she entered the shop. "I need to talk to you!"

The manager of the Bargain Dragons Centre, still in his outdoor coat, held his hands up like buffers. "Wo! Wo! Good morning, Caron, take a deep breath, will you?"

"I need to talk!"

This was not the way Dav planned to start his day. Caron's rushes of blood were becoming increasingly wearisome. "Caron," he said, "what you need to do is calm down."

"What's up?" Dobbin had appeared from the tea room.

"It's private," said Caron.

"Go on, Dobbin," said Dav. "Make yourself scarce. Sit down, Caron, for God's sake."

Caron sat down. She had barely slept and was hyperventilating. Dobbin returned to the tea room and Dav took off his coat. "So what's got your goat?" he asked.

"They're killing the dragons," blurted Caron.

"Who is?"

"Batman and Robin! They're making them fight! Making them kill each other!"

Dav frowned. "How do you know this?" he asked.

"I've seen it!"

"Where?"

"At the old Skylarks holiday park. In the swimming pool. Dav, it's vile, there were hundreds of people there."

"So you've seen this?"

Caron faltered. "I know about it," she replied.

"How do you know about it?"

"A tip off," she said.

"Who from?"

"Someone," said Caron. Her lack of sleep had rendered her incapable of formulating a simple lie.

"Someone," repeated Dav.

"Does it matter?"

"You know where it is, you know how many people were there, but you haven't seen it."

Caron could feel the blush coming over her face. Her natural honesty made her a hopeless liar. "What if I have?" she said.

Dav drew back in his chair. "You didn't find this by accident, did you?" he said.

Caron remained silent.

"So you tracked them."

Caron did not deny it.

"And the only way you could have done that is by using one of our trackers."

Caron's guilt was plain. "Does it matter?" she said.

"Yes, Caron, it does matter! Because those trackers belong to the shop, and if you took one, that is theft!"

"I didn't take it. It was attached to the cage."

"What, and you left it on there by accident?"

Again, Caron's face betrayed her.

"Do you realise what would happen if customers found out we'd been spying on them? This shop would be finished!"

"But they're killing dragons, Dav! The dragons we sell them!"

"Caron, we are not responsible for what customers do with the dragons."

"Don't you care?"

"It makes no difference if I care or not, Caron. We're sellers, not social workers."

"You don't care."

"I care that I've got a job."

"And nothing else matters."

"Do you want to feed my kids?"

Caron was not going to get into that discussion.

"You told me once," she said, steadying herself, "if customers cause problems, we can ban them. So why don't we just ban Batman and Robin?"

"What good would that do? They'd just send someone else in to buy for them. And anyway, how do you know all the other customers aren't doing the same thing? Let's face it, second quality dragons are pretty much useless."

"Then we've got to stop the dragon fights!"

"You'll never do that."

Caron's eyes narrowed. "You know about them!" she said.

"I may have heard rumours. But the fact is, it's legal."

"If you knew about this, why didn't you tell me?"

"Because it's nothing to do with you, Caron! If you were selling furniture, and people were chopping it up for firewood, that's nothing to do with you!"

"Dragons aren't furniture!"

"No, fair enough, furniture is useful."

Caron's heart pumped hard. The red mist was on her. "You. . .are lower than vermin," she said.

Dav's face turned to stone. He pulled open his desk drawer, took out a manual, and found the page he was looking for.

"'Unauthorised removal of shop property,'" he quoted. "'Unless a good reason is given, standard disciplinary procedures will always apply.'" Dav closed the manual, dropped it in the drawer, and slammed the drawer shut. "Well done, Caron," he said. "You're on a red warning."

Ten

Caron sat in the bedroom of her small flat, deep in thought. She'd worked so hard to make it a home, a cosy place, not like that sterile industrial unit that Jac Dekker lived in. Not for the first time her mind replayed the night when her father had ordered her out of the family home, destroying in an instant everything that had given her security. Again and again he'd repeated the phrase "I just want you out of my sight," while his mother sat like a shop window mannequin refusing to take sides. How weak she'd been, how useless as a mother: Caron would rather die than end up like that.

Nor in a million years would Caron crawl back to her father and beg his forgiveness. She had done nothing wrong, other than argue the toss with narrow-minded teachers. The irony was that she loved learning. But only learning what she wanted to learn, in the way that she wanted to learn it. Caron was interested in so many things, most of which meant nothing to her teachers or her parents. And once she got her own place, she began filling it with articles which inspired her: an Afghan rug from a night market, a Balinese mosaic mirror, a hand-painted bee candle holder made by her friend Rosa. Bit by bit she turned two sparsely furnished rooms into a magical place, like a mini theatre.

Now Caron imagined all those treasured possessions dumped on the landing as she desperately fought to turn her key in the changed lock. Not a paranoid fantasy: exactly what happened to the last junior seller when he arrived home from being sacked. Exactly, no doubt, what had happened to Max Williams.

So what could she do?

She made a list:

Councillors/MPs

Friends/Activists

Local media

Social media – make video?

NSPA - National Society for the Protection of Animals

There were potential problems everywhere. Caron had never approached an elected politician in her life and her instinct was to trust none of them. She did trust her friends, at least most of them, but not many would be prepared to put themselves on the line, and those who might, the ones involved in campaigning groups, worried her: Bel, for example, who'd been duped by a police agent and was actually living with him when he was exposed: one reason why she'd never go to the police either.

Of course, she could go it alone, as she so often did: she knew how to shoot and edit a video, she could put it online anonymously, but it could still be traced to her. Far better if she could persuade someone else to do it. Surely it was NSPA's job to deal with these things? If she rang them, they did not need to know who she was, and in any case, they surely would not reveal the source of their information.

Caron took the plunge.

"I want to report some serious animal cruelty," she said, as steadily as she could manage.

"Is this something you've personally witnessed?" It was a woman's voice, adult, reassuring.

"Yes."

"Ok. Try to give me as much detail as possible."

Caron felt a gush of relief. Someone who would listen! She began recounting the events of the night before, increasingly breathless, unable to hide her emotion. When she finished there was a long pause.

"I'm sorry," said the voice.

"Sorry?"

"We have heard about this."

"Oh."

"There's nothing we can do."

"What?"

"It's not illegal."

"Are you sure?". Caron had already heard this from Dav, of course, but had been sure it couldn't be true.

"The legislation against cruelty to animals is quite specific. Much of it was passed a long time ago. You must realise that to previous generations, the dragon was a mythical creature. No-one imagined the scientific advances which would lead to it becoming real. We do care about this issue, of course. We want to see a change in the law but, frankly, the chances are not good."

"Why?"

"That's not for me to say."

"Why not?"

"Bear in mind, for hundreds of years they chased foxes with dogs and broke the necks of horses in steeplechases."

"So what's the point of you?" Caron was angry with the woman now. She ended the call before there was any reply, threw herself down on the bed and spent ten minutes in a sea of despair before jumping up, filling a small copper watering can and feeding the planter of violas on her windowsill. Caron loved the bright optimistic faces of these dainty flowers: they always gave her a little hope. No, she was not alone. There were good people out there. That journalist, for example. The one who wrote the article about the sea defences. What was his name?

Caron checked the bookmarks on her laptop: yes, there was the article. The journalist's name was Elis Jones and his email address was provided. Of course it was a risk to use this old-fashioned and insecure means of communication, but there was no need to reveal the real reason why she was contacting him. She had simply read his article and had some information which he urgently needed to know. No need to reply, just ring her on Faultline. Faultline was massively expensive but supposedly secure.

Or was it? By now Caron was desperately tired, and the moment the email was sent she wanted to get it back, but of course that was impossible. So she sent another, asking him to ignore the first one and not under any circumstances to ring her, only to get an immediate automated reply that his mailbox was full.

Half an hour later, the notification came. He was ringing her.

Caron ignored it.

He rang again.

Clearly he had believed what she had said: her message was urgent. He was ringing her in good faith: she had to answer.

"Hello?" she said.

"It's Elis Jones," came the reply. "You messaged me." The voice was soft and sympathetic. It reminded her of Mr Cummins. Immediately her fears and suspicions were overtaken by a desperate desire to unload her emotions. Out it came, the whole story, with barely a gap for him to acknowledge he was listening. But his response at the end made it quite clear that she had struck a chord with him.

"We need to meet," he said.

"Ok," she replied.

"Do you know the Brazil Café?"

"Yes."

"Tomorrow at seven?"

"Ok. . .I'll be wearing a blue coat."

"I'll see you there."

Eleven

aron was dreading going to work now. The atmosphere
had changed since she'd blurted out that insult: no more
chummy sarcasm from Dav, just instructions, delivered acidly,
without a trace of humour. Humour was important to Caron:
jokey, sometimes quite brutal, sparring was normal in her
friendships, so despite all the things she could see wrong with
her manager, she had still felt a kind of kinship with him.

She did consider apologising. But Caron rarely, if ever, apol-
ogised. That, again, was the legacy of her bullying father, and
her determination never to show weakness. So she rejected this
idea, which would make it look like she was in the wrong,
not Dav. If he cared nothing about the dragons, and when she
thought of dragons she inevitably thought of Blaze, then he really was what she'd called him.

So Caron walked in next morning prepared to be as distant
as Dav, to not even say hello unless maybe he did. Except he
didn't. He simply greeted her with the words, "Got a job for
you."

"What?" she replied.

"Dump your things in the tea room. Then follow me."

Caron left her bag, and coat, as requested, and returned, not knowing what to expect.

"We've had a death," said Dav.

"A dragon?"

"Follow me."

Dav beckoned Caron after him and marched in his foot-thumping way down the shop. *Be prepared*, thought Caron, though she scarcely knew how. In her mind they were on a beeline to Blaze's cage, but no, thank God, it was the next one along. The little dragon lay on its side, stock still, eyes half open.

"What happened?" asked Caron.

"Failed experiment," replied Dav.

"What?"

"The old man decided to try out some kind of magic potion. It was supposed to brighten its colours. I came in this morning and this was the result."

Dav viewed the dead dragon. Caron couldn't.

"Sad, isn't it?" said Dav.

Caron did not respond. How could Dav care about this dead dragon and not about all those who died so horribly in fights? Was he being sarcastic? Caron thought to say the dragon had at least escaped a worse fate, but thought the better of it. Instead she said, "He won't try it again, will he?"

"Not if I have anything to do with it."

"He could have done it in Ruby Street."

"Some hope. You know how the old man treats this place. It's his dumping ground."

Was this an attempt to find common ground, make friends again? Caron could not read what was going on.

"What are you going to do with it?" she asked.

"Better chuck it on the barbie."

"What, me?"

"Yes, you!"

The 'barbie' was Dav's slang for the incinerator which stood in the little back yard behind the shop. Every time Jac Dekker was away for a few days Dav would use it to get rid of a few unsaleable items, but Caron had never been asked to burn a dead body before.

"Can't Dobbin do it?"

"He's busy."

"Doing what?"

"Never you mind."

"I can't do it."

"You better."

It crossed Caron's mind that this whole situation could be a set-up. The dragon's death might be nothing to do with Dekker; Dav could have arranged it as a kind of revenge.

"I need to go to the toilet," she said.

Dav ignored the request. He began telling Caron a story about Danny, her predecessor, and his love of starting fires, one of which nearly burnt down the shop. She'd never asked much about Danny, but he was the seller who'd lost his job and found his possessions on the landing.

"Can I go to the toilet, please?" she repeated, but again Dav ignored her, and continued the story of Danny, whether she wanted to hear it or not.

"He was a bit of a sad sack, Danny. He really thought he was the big man in his pinstripe suit but to be honest he was a laughingstock. Then his girlfriend dumped him and he went postal. Started missing days, saying he had the dentist and things, but it was rubbish. He never even had a dentist."

"How do you know?"

"How do I know anything? Haven't you noticed, I am God in this shop?"

"Yes, I have noticed."

"So he lost his job, lost his flat, and next thing we know, he's breaking in and sleeping In the shop."

Caron was feeling increasingly uneasy. It did not sit right that Dav was chatting to her like this, as if suddenly things were fine between them and she was not in immediate danger of going the same way as Danny. She'd worked in the store for months and Dav had never told her about her predecessor before.

"I really do need the toilet," she said.

"Ok. After you've done the cremation."

"Can't Dobbin do it?"

"I've asked you to do it."

Throughout this conversation Caron had avoided turning her eyes to the next cage along, Blaze's cage. She just knew the little dragon would be aware of the death of its neighbour.

All dragons, even the second quality ones, had a strong sense of smell, partly through their darting tongues. Blaze would be filled with panic at the scent of death. All its instincts would be telling it to flee. But as there was no way to do so, the panic would only intensify, to an unbearable level. And if it saw her carrying the corpse, how would that affect its view of her? That she was some kind of predator, responsible for the death?

"Caron," said Dav. "I'm ordering you to do it."

"I need the toilet," said Caron, yet again.

"You'll have to wait."

"I can't wait!"

Caron marched back down the shop, heedless of Dav's reaction, and threw open the tearoom door. Dobbin looked up, startled. His hand was inside her shoulder bag.

"What are you doing?" she snapped.

"I wanted to see the make," blurted Dobbin. "I was going to get my girlfriend one."

"What girlfriend? You haven't even got a girlfriend!"

"Yes I have."

"*What were you doing in my bag?*"

"I told you."

Caron seized her bag, looked inside to see if anything was missing, then scanned the room, saw Dobbin's coat, marched over and started rifling through the pockets.

"Hey!" he yelled.

"See how you like it!"

Dobbin grabbed the coat and ripped it from Caron's hands. Caron grabbed it back and for a moment the threat of serious violence hung in the air. Then Dav arrived.

"Wo!" he cried. "What's going on?"

"You tell me!" cried Caron. "I'm sure you know!"

"Know what?"

"Know why he's going through my bag!"

Dav looked to Dobbin. "I told her," he said. "I was trying to find out what make it was."

"Then why didn't you just ask me?"

"Didn't want to bother you."

"What rubbish! What were you looking for really?"

No reply. Caron stood there heaving, like a raft in a storm. She felt violated.

"I thought you needed the toilet," said Dav.

Caron took her bag and pointedly put it over her shoulder before locking herself into the toilet cubicle and double-checking that all her personal effects were still there. Often Mr Cummins would joke with her that she was a bit paranoid, and yes, she did tend to believe that people were plotting against her, but didn't this just prove she was right? She would never trust anyone who worked for Dekkers again.

Twelve

The Brazil Café was well known to Caron. She had spent many afternoons there, meeting Rosa or Beti or Elf when she should have been at school. It was also a place she would sit, sometimes for hours, with a single cup of coffee, in the weeks after being thrown out of home. It was a time she preferred not to think about, sleeping on different sofas, worrying if she had outstayed her welcome, or had been welcome in the first place. Friendships were different when you were in dire straits.

Then there was the night she'd found herself out on the street. How different the town seemed with all security taken away. How careless were the people, so intent on their own business, so blind to her obvious need. She'd finally taken shelter in the stairwell of a block of flats, out of the wind and rain but with no more comfort than cold concrete. What she would have done then for the warmth of any living thing, for the company of even a small bedraggled dragon.

So what kind of company would Elis Jones provide? He had an old-fashioned name, but his voice sounded relatively young. Caron's nerves were tinged with – what was that word that Mr Cummins had used? *Frisson*. A frisson of excitement.

Caron checked her phone. Five past seven. Five past seven, and the café door was opening!

Oh no!

What was the chances of that?

Farah!

Caron took a sudden and intense interest in a framed print of Rio de Janeiro on the wall. All in vain.

"Caron, hi!"

Caron wheeled round. "What are you doing here?" she snapped. She had not intended to sound so hostile, but meeting Elis was challenge enough and she simply could not cope with the situation.

"Pardon me for breathing," said Farah.

"Sorry, I've got things on my mind."

"What's that then?"

"It's private."

"Oo, top secret, is it?"

What was it with Farah? Was she autistic, or was there some other reason she could not read, or did not want to read, the signs on Caron's face?

"It's private," she repeated, more forcefully.

Farah viewed her with puzzlement. "Am I being too forward?" she asked.

"Yes," said Caron.

"Sorry, love. That's me all over. I've been told it's fear of rejection. See, love, when I was a kid I couldn't run around with the others, never learnt how to socialise properly."

Caron was flummoxed. It was so much a part of her nature to help people, especially those with disadvantages, that it now seemed impossible to ask Farah to go away. But the café door was opening and a man was coming in: the way his eyes roved round the room made it clear he was looking for someone and yes, his eyes focussed on Caron's blue coat.

There was no escape from the situation. Caron raised a hand to confirm he'd got the right person and the man came over. He looked about thirty, old fashioned blue denim shirt, matching pale blue eyes, dark curly hair. Quite good-looking, but rather uncertain, edgy.

"I'm Elis," he said. His eyes were going left-right, left-right, from Caron to Farah, who was equally curious.

"This is Farah," said Caron. "Farah's worried about the tidal surge." She had remembered the discussion in the second-hand warehouse.

"Right," said Elis, clearly uncomfortable.

"This man wrote an article about it," Caron explained to Farah. "He's a journalist."

"Really?" said Farah.

"Yes, the tidal defences they're building, it's all a rip off, this councillor's family got the contract, nothing's being done about it. . ." Caron was aware of the hot flush climbing up her neck – could it be seen? Was it obvious she didn't know what she was talking about?

Someone else say something!

"Do you mind if I sit down?" asked Farah.

Caron hesitated. If she told Farah that she and Elis were having a private meeting it would surely arouse her suspicions. But if she allowed Farah to sit next to her it would signal to Elis that she was in on the meeting. And if she pretended she hadn't heard, Farah would soon be in pain: she could not stand still for long.

Caron fell back on her lifelong habit: when in doubt, sound as confident as possible. "I'll tell you what," she said. "You have my seat. I'll go and get some coffees. Would you like a coffee, Elis?"

"Oh. Yes, OK. Thanks."

"Farah?"

"Won't say no, love. Thank you very much".

"Right. I'll need a hand. Could you give me a hand, please, Elis?"

It was a good move: isolating Elis, Caron would be able to explain that Farah was not an ally. She jumped up and strode over to the counter as certain as a supermodel, Elis dutifully following. She then made a great play of reading the board displaying all the alternative coffees on sale, though in reality her head was shot and it might as well have been written in Chinese.

The delay was fatal. Just as she turned to engage Elis in the crucial conversation, she felt a tap on her shoulder.

Farah!

"Actually love, I'll just have a cannolo. I don't mind paying for it."

How had she moved so fast? Was it by chance she was preventing Caron having a private word with Elis? Did she somehow know what was going on?

What was certain was that she was not going away. The coffees and the cannoli were ordered, they returned to their seats, and Farah launched into an animated account of a blog she'd read detailing which areas of Llantresedd were most at risk of flooding: Toadstool Lane for sure, but not Ruby Street, or Chapel Lane, so Caron's flat would be spared: actually a disturbing piece of information, as it revealed Farah knew where Caron's flat was, although she'd never been invited there.

Elis's eyes were once again going left-right between Caron and Farah. He clearly had little interest in what Farah was saying. Eventually he downed his coffee in one gulp and said, "Are we going to talk about the dragons?"

"What's this?" said Farah.

"The dragon fights."

Farah's eyes shot to Caron's. "There's been some fighting," blurted Caron. "In the shop."

"In the shop?" repeated Elis.

"When was there fighting in the shop?" asked Farah.

"I shouldn't have made so much of it," said Caron.

"It's the first I've heard of it," said Farah.

The blush that had been creeping up on Caron now took full hold. She did not need a mirror to know that she was blood red. What was Elis thinking of her? That she was a stupid girl, stupid like her father always said, a stupid attention-seeker wasting the time of a busy professional man.

It was like one of those dreams where you suddenly realise you are naked.

Without another word, Caron fled.

Thirteen

Caron cursed herself for arranging the meeting with Elis, for laying herself open like that, risking such humiliation. Of course Farah had turned up. Wasn't it obvious by now that she was a spy? Had it been by chance that she had also turned up at the second-hand warehouse, asking all those questions? Just because she was disabled didn't mean she was trustworthy. On the contrary, being disabled helped her avoid suspicion, especially to someone like Caron who rooted for outsiders.

There remained the question of how Farah knew Caron would be at the Café Brazil, and if she also knew who Caron was going to meet. Did she eavesdrop on the phone call? Access Caron's email or even Faultline? It was not safe to use any of these methods of communication. Not that Caron was thinking of contacting Elis Jones again. She wanted to forget the whole episode.

The upcoming flood, however, she could not ignore. The tidal surge was now predicted for the following evening. Every news channel reported it, even Patriot News, who said these things had always happened, and people should ignore what the oceanographers were saying.

Fortunately, there were more reliable sources of information: all pretty much agreed with what Farah had said, that Caron's flat and Ruby Street would be safe, but that the lower reaches of town, including Toadstool Lane, were certain to be underwater. If the waters were up one metre, it could knock people of their feet and flood the bottom floors of buildings; if it reached two metres it could carry cars, trees and signs away, which would act as battering rams balls causing massive extra damage; and if it reached three, it would be up to the first floor of buildings, making almost everywhere unsafe. Power lines would come down, gas and electric would be cut off, people without mobility could well die.

Caron's mind went back to Elfin – Elf – for so long her best friend. They were alike in many ways – both interested in music, politics and weird funny things, both impossible to teach. Elf was equally determined to do things his own way. He was a nice-looking boy, with an open, lively face under a mop of uncontrollable curls, but she was not attracted to him and he said he was not attracted to her. So they got along easily, though anyone who did not understand their sense of humour would have thought they hated each other: they loved to spar, to wind each other up, but it was all rough play.

Or was it? No-one would have called Elf a macho man, but there was a macho streak in him when it came to scares like the Brenner virus or the melting of the ice caps. He didn't like showing fear, and apparently jokingly would construct elaborate theories as to why the scientists' views were just a con to deliberately scare people. If there were no giant icebergs break-ing away in the past, how come the Titanic hit one? And how come no one realised the real cause of major heatwaves were the number of mirrors on Earth, rather than the number of cars and planes?

It was amusing enough at first, but as the months went by the joke began to wear off on Caron. It got increasingly tire-some to have to defend herself every time she used sun block or refused to buy products containing palm oil. And bit by bit she became convinced Elf was starting to believe the nonsense he was not only foisting on her but everybody else they knew. One night a supposed play fight turned onto something a lot more serious, something on the verge of violence. Given her experi-ences with her dad, Caron did not take lightly to this. She shut the door on Elf and did not answer next time he came round. In return he defriended her all over social media and wrote a little song about it all which inevitably she got to hear. So her best friend had joined an increasing army of enemies, and her insecurities grew accordingly.

The upcoming flood would certainly test how serious were Elf's views. His flat was right in the firing line.

Jac Dekker, needless to say, was no eco-warrior. But he was a hard-headed businessman, and even if the meteorologists were wrong, he was taking no risks. As Caron arrived for work next day, the vans were already outside the Toadstool Lane store, shipping out the breath converters, the foodstuffs and other sundries, even Dav's managerial office chair.

Dav seemed to be enjoying the experience. He didn't often have a small army to order about, rather than just Caron and Dobbin, but he was doing it with his usual brusque good humour, joking with the drivers, threatening the van boys' shins with his favourite pebble if they moved too slowly. He had clearly decided to pretend the fight between Caron and Dobbin had never happened.

"Morning, Caz," he said, brightly. "Don't take off your coat, you're clearing the tearoom."

Caron complied without discussion. She had not forgotten, nor would ever forget, that Dav had purposely waylaid her while Dobbin was searching her bag. She would keep her conversations with him to a minimum and as far as possible ignore her co-worker altogether.

One glance at the tearoom showed her that Dobbin was not intending to apologise or make the peace. The random arrangement of mugs and jars around the kettle had been carefully subdivided, so that even Caron's possessions kept their distance from Dobbin's, as if her slightly alternative hot drinks would infect his coffee. How petty, she thought, but if he wanted a war, he had better be prepared for the consequences.

Caron got to work clearing the furniture. She was strong for her size, as much through determination as her wiry arms: strong enough to take the small table as well as the chairs. Just as well, as she no more wanted to ask for help from the van boys as Dobbin. But though she seized the opportunity to lose herself in routine manual work, she could not ignore the question now dominating her mind. What was to happen to the dragons? As yet, their cages remained unmoved.

By lunchtime all the stock and furniture had been cleared, the wind was rising and it seemed as if the whole world was on the move. Everything hidden away inside the houses of lower Llantresedd was now out on the street, the shops and cafes were boarded up and sandbagged, an endless trail of vehicles were heading out of town. Yet Dav had still given no instructions regarding Blaze and its companions. Nor had anyone ventured over the road to the warehouse where the secondhand creatures were stored. Caron was getting increasingly anxious. A conversation with her manager was unavoidable.

"What's happening to the dragons?" she asked.

Dav tapped his nose.

"What, can't you tell me?" said Caron.

"You don't want to know."

"I do want to know."

"The old man's no fool, Caron. He's fully insured against flood damage."

"What do you mean?"

"I mean, if anything should happen to the dragons, he'll get full market value from the insurance company."

Caron's jaw dropped. "Are you saying he's leaving them here?"

Dav did not deny it.

"You can't be serious!"

"I'm deadly serious, Caz."

Caron stared in disbelief. Dav held her stare for a few moments, then cracked into a smile.

"Take a chill pill, Caz!" he said. "The old man may be ruthless, but he's got a reputation to think of! You know everyone in this town thinks he's flipping Santa!"

"That wasn't funny."

"You used to have a sense of humour."

"So what is happening to them?"

"He's made a deal with a shop in Arfon Wells. The manager will be here soon. He's going to look over the stock and if he's happy he's going to take them."

This was no great relief to Caron. She had known a time would come when she would be parted from Blaze, but she'd held out some hope that the little dragon would not be going far. Arfon Wells was almost a hundred miles away.

"Tell you what, Caz. You can help me show him round. Use some of your female charm on him."

As it happened, the manager of the other store was a woman. Caron took to her immediately. There was nothing high-handed or bossy about Jane Fratelli: she was a neat, purposeful woman who had none of the shiftiness of Jac Dekker. She addressed Caron as well as Dav when she spoke to them and looked both in the eyes. But she made it very clear she was there on business and not to waste time on small talk.

The three went over to the secondhand warehouse. Jane Fratelli was not impressed by the slippery metal steps to this: surely a danger, especially in winter? Dav was dismissive.

Caron sensed this woman was making him feel insecure; her attachment to her grew all the more.

The three progressed around the cages, Dav talking up the sad specimens, Jane assessing them with a cool scientific eye. Caron was getting more and more excited being around her. Could Caron maybe have her own shop one day? Memories of selling homemade lemonade from the front garden with her childhood friend Maya came back to her. What a thrill it was to get a customer, or to count the coins at the end of the afternoon! And how good it would be now to be her own boss, to only sell responsibly sourced goods, at a fair price, and treat her staff as equals! Fired up with the thought of this, Caron weighed into the sales pitch, mentioning the creatures, just like the ones they were viewing, which she had sold to satisfied customers.

Jane listened but did not react.

When the viewing was over, Jane gave her judgement.

"I'm sorry," she said. "I can't take any of these."

Dav and Caron were equally gutted.

"I thought that was part of the deal," said Dav.

"No, no. I've only agreed to take the dragons, providing they're in saleable condition. I did say I would look at the other stock, but frankly, with the space they'll take up, taking these would never be cost-effective."

"Then what are we going to do with them?" said Caron, wheeling on Dav.

"We'll discuss that later," replied Dav. He shot Caron a look which said "that's enough."

But Caron was not only concerned about the creatures in the warehouse. As they crossed back to the shop, Jane's clinical eye, which Caron had so admired, was beginning to look a threat. She would surely notice Blaze's withered wing.

So much was at stake. If the dragons got a new lease of life in Arfon Wells, there would surely be no dragon fighting there, and the dynamic duo would surely not travel that far to buy them. And even if they did, surely Jane, unlike Dav, would refuse to sell to obvious criminals, especially if she'd been warned about them. Yes, maybe she'd even take up the fight against them? She'd surely give them something to think about!

But would she take a damaged dragon?

Dav was clearly worried about all the dragons.

"They're small," he said, "but they're good sellers."

"I know what they're like," was Jane's curt reply. She was efficiently examining each one with her eyes, assessing it, then moving on. From the little nods of her head, Caron guessed she was ok with what she'd seen. But bit by bit they were approaching Blaze's cage.

Maybe Caron could distract her at the vital moment?

No, that would be too obvious.

But, saints be praised, not necessary. Blaze was backed up into the corner of the cage, its withered wing out of view. *You clever creature*, thought Caron, but swiftly avoided its eyesight. She did not want Blaze coming to life and hobbling towards her.

Jane viewed Blaze for what seemed an age. Was she responding to its charisma, just as Caron had? If so, would it matter if she saw its wing? Maybe she would love it just like Caron did! Maybe she would invite both of them to live with her in Arfon Wells!

For now, Jane said nothing. That was good enough, that she hadn't suspected any problem. They continued to the last few dragons, then she gave her verdict.

"I'll take them," she said.

"Fantastic," said Dav, while Caron fought the urge to throw her arms around Jane and cry with thanks.

"When can you deliver?" asked Jane.

"I'll fix that right away," said Dav. "Dobbin!"

Dobbin, who Caron had managed to avoid all morning, ambled up the shop.

"Any vans free, Dobs?" asked Dav.

"Matt should be back shortly," replied Dobbin.

"Ok, soon as he's back, get this lot loaded. They're off to Arfon Wells."

"What, even the one with the wonky wing?"

Caron was thunderstruck. Either Dobbin was beyond stupid or he knew exactly what he was doing. Did he really hate Caron so much he wanted to see her favourite dragon die? It wasn't her fault they gave her the Ruby Street gig ahead of him!

There was, of course, no possibility that his flippant comment would pass Jane Fratelli by.

"Which dragon are we talking about?" she asked.

"The wing's just a bit different," said Dav. "It's a very good dragon otherwise."

"Can you show me which one please?"

Dav duly led Jane to Blaze's cage. As chance would have it, Blaze was now looking straight ahead, both wings visible. It seemed unspeakably poignant to Caron, Blaze having his disability assessed. It was an exam it could never pass, no matter how hard it tried.

"It's a fantastic dragon," she found herself saying. "I think it's the best in the shop."

"Yes, well that's your opinion, Caron," replied Dav, swiftly. "Just to reassure you, Mrs Fratelli, this is the only dragon which is handicapped in any way."

Handicapped. What a horrible description that was. It completely undercut what Caron had just said, and she could tell by the expression on Jane's face that it would not help her reach a kind verdict.

"I'm sorry," she said. "I can't take this one."

"It will sell, honestly," protested Caron.

"That may be," replied Jane. "But it's a matter of principle. Mr Dekker assured me that no dragons were ill or injured."

"It's not an injury!" protested Caron.

"That's enough, Caron," said Dav. "Mrs Fratelli has made her decision. You can start lifting the cages to the front of the shop ready for the van."

Fourteen

With all but one of the dragons gone, the Bargain Dragons Centre was a desolate place. Caron knew the flood would only be temporary, but it felt like the end of the world. And her encounter with Jane Fratelli had unsettled her as much as all the upsetting events of the past week. She had hardened herself to living alone, to making her own way, to ignoring the mother who had been so useless to her. But now she realised how much she craved an older woman to whom she could turn, someone to comfort her in her distress, someone who would understand those things she cared about so much.

But Jane had not come to Toadstool Lane to look after Caron, and despite her intelligence and her down-to-earth, apparently reasonable nature, she was devoted to profit, not little dragons. So again it was down to Caron, Caron alone, to care for the creature.

She asked Dav what the plans for the last remaining dragon were.

"It'll have to go over the road with the others," he replied.

"What, you're leaving them over there?"

"They'll have food and water."

"They'll have water alright!"

"The flood's not going up that high."

"How do you know?"

"Caron, I'm following every bulletin. They're predicting two metres. Nowhere near the first floor."

"If they're telling the truth."

"Jeez, Caron, are you paranoid? Why are they going to lie about it?"

"To keep us scared."

"Why? Why do they want to keep us scared?"

"So they can control us."

Caron was not even convincing herself with this argument; it was something Elf used to say, possibly to wind her up. But the thought of Blaze helplessly trapped as the waters slowly rose was impossible to face.

"Why did Dobbin have to open his stupid mouth?" she said.

"That's enough," said Dav.

"Seriously, she would have taken all the dragons if he hadn't blabbed like an idiot!"

"It's done. That's enough."

"He did it on purpose!"

"You really are paranoid."

Caron calmed herself. If she started saying all the things that were on her mind, Dobbin having a vendetta against her and Farah being a company spy, she could be facing a swift exit.

"Surely," she said, "there must be a place we can put one dragon. What about Jac Dekker's house?"

"No hope."

"Why not? It's huge."

"Yes, Caz, but it's his home, not a zoo."

"What, is it too much hard work for him?"

Dav's expression hardened. "Listen, Caz," he said. "Whatever you think of the old man, he is not afraid of hard work. Back in the day, everyone got their solar panels from China. No-one could compete with them on price. So the old man started making them himself. That's how he started this business. Working day and night. Then when dragons came along, and everyone said they were just a gimmick, he invested in them. Sold them all himself, didn't have suckers like us back then."

"On poverty wages"

"You'd have no wage at all if it weren't for him. He was the first boss in this town to employ you kids."

Caron ignored the insult. Getting into an argument like this was not helping Blaze.

"I still don't see why we can't find a home for that dragon," she said.

"Are you offering?"

Until this point, it had not even occurred to Caron that she could take Blaze home. The thought filled her with a surge of optimism.

"Ok," she said.

"On second thoughts," said Dav, "I don't think that would be a good idea."

"Why not?"

"You're too flaky, Caz. You'll probably do a runner with it."

"What, and lose my job, and my flat? I'm not going to do that."

"No, if anything goes wrong, I'll take the rap for it."

"Nothing's going to go wrong! Dav, you go mad when there's no customers and we're just standing around. But now I'm going to go home and do nothing for maybe a week. Doesn't it make sense for me to have a job to do?"

Dav pondered. Caron had clearly hit the right note.

"How would you get it home?" he asked.

"Can't one of the vans take it?"

"Then everyone will know. I'd rather they didn't."

"I could ask someone, but. . ."

Did Caron know anyone who had a car? Her mind had gone blank. There was her dad of course but. . .no, she could not ask him, even for this.

"Ok, listen," said Dav. "I will take you. But don't forget you owe me."

Fifteen

The journey back to Caron's flat was not a long one: that time she caught a bus it took ten minutes. But this was no ordinary day. The roads were jam-packed with cars, vans and e-scooters as all the residents of the low-lying streets made their escape from the upcoming flood. And even though Caron spent almost every day in the company of her manager, being trapped in a passenger seat next to him was a new and uncomfortable experience. Was that a bit sinister, that thing he'd said about her owing him, or was she being paranoid again? And how could she just make small talk, knowing she was on a red warning and he held her future in his hands?

Caron glanced again and again over her shoulder. Should there have been a seatbelt around Blaze's cage? The little dragon had retreated to the back of it, so it was impossible to tell how it was reacting to this change of circumstances. But Caron wished Dav would turn down his music, the thumping bass from which was surely not calming the dragon's nerves. Nor did Caron share Dav's enthusiasm for soul music of the 1970s.

The traffic was barely moving. They could be half an hour yet. Caron would have to try to make conversation.

"So where do you live then, Dav?" she asked.

"That," said Dav, "is a state secret."

"Only making conversation."

Dav sang a snatch of the song they were listening to: *The First, The Last, My Everything.*

"Like this stuff, do you?" said Caron.

"Barry White, Caz. Back in the day he was a big name. They called him the Walrus of Love."

"Identify with him, do you?"

Caron winced. What a stupid thing to say! It was the kind of banter she'd have with a close friend, not her manager. But Dav did not seem unduly bothered.

"You'd have to ask the wife," he replied.

How Caron hated that phrase.

"Does the wife have a name?" she asked.

"Mrs Montague."

Caron's attempts to relax the atmosphere was having the opposite effect. She resolved to say no more. Dav's refusal to reveal any personal information, while on the way to her most private place, was fuelling her suspicions. Was his real intention to check out her flat, to see maybe if it was full of leaflets from some kind of animal liberation group? Or other clues as to where she was really at?

Well, there were no leaflets. If Dav knew anything about Caron, he would be aware that she had never joined any kind of group, even a social group, for fear other people would make her do something she didn't want to. The same reason she found her job so difficult.

Thankfully the traffic did not reach a complete standstill, and at last the journey came to an end. Caron and Dav carried the cage into 25, Chapel Lane and up the stairs to the door of flat 2a.

"I can manage from here," said Caron.

"I don't think so, Caron," said Dav. "Come on, open the door."

Reluctantly Caron complied. There was, she reassured herself, nothing to hide in her flat. But the moment the door opened she realised how untidy it was, and although she felt this shouldn't matter, she could not help feeling embarrassed. Dav let out a little 'blimey' at the sight of it, to which she instantly responded by saying she didn't have 'the wife' to keep it tidy. Then she realised, to her even greater embarrassment, that the photo of Blaze was still on the wall.

Dav saw it. "You've got a *photo* of this dragon?" he said.

"And?" she replied.

"That's a bit weird."

"I don't think so."

Dav's face was full of suspicion. Inevitably his eyes started roving round the room, just as she had feared, in search of other insights into her secret life.

"Can we put this down please?" she said.

"Ok. Where do you want it?"

"Under the window."

They lowered the cage into the desired position, just below the quivering violas. Then Caron hustled Dav out of her flat, rather more aggressively than she'd intended, but by now she was stressed beyond reason: she felt as if she'd been burgled. Nor did she need advice about looking after Blaze, or to be reminded to keep up with messages about her return to work. As her parting comment made clear, she was not an idiot.

But never mind, never mind: there was a light breeze through the partly opened window, the violas were as beautiful as ever, and Blaze was in her flat! Caron's heart was bursting with excitement: it was like that scene in *Wuthering Heights* when Catherine and Heathcliff were at last together: except the intensity of that encounter led to Catherine's death, and Caron seriously wondered if the same might happen to her. To have this creature's life in her hands was a daunting responsibility.

"Welcome home, Blaze."

It was the moment Caron had been waiting for. She carefully unlatched the cage door and eased it open. In her mind, many times, she had rehearsed the next scene: the little dragon peering curiously into her room, then hopping out to explore every nook and crannie, its appetite for life beyond the cage knowing no bounds.

But the scene never happened. Blaze stayed hunched in the corner of its cage, only its eyes exploring the new surroundings, without much interest.

"Come on, Blaze, you're safe here."

Still no response. Should she reach in and touch it, stroke it? Would that reassure it, or make it more anxious? Could it even bite her, or rake her with its claws? Most creatures would fight if they felt threatened, or literally cornered.

No, she wouldn't risk that. Far better to tempt it out. She'd brought home a few eggsticks as treats for Blaze, and laid one of these just outside of the cage. That caught Blaze's attention: the tip of its tongue appeared and ran across its upper lip. But no, the desire was not enough to overcome the fear.

Caron decided it was best to give it time. The wind and rain were picking up, so she shut the window, turned on her laptop and checked out the local news channel. The tidal surge had begun: the new defences, still incomplete, had been overwhelmed and there was frightening footage of massive waves tossing boats into the harbour walls. Six people had been killed taking selfies from the lifeboat station. Numerous streets were now canals, cars were being swept away and worse was to come.

Nothing seemed secure anymore. Was Caron's flat really safe? Did Blaze have some kind of instinct that that the predictions were wrong and disaster was imminent? That seemed far-fetched, but really, people knew so little about dragons. They had virtually been created by AI and could be compared to no other life-form on Earth. They did not even have a natural habitat. Was it such a surprise that Blaze did not want to leave its cage when it had known nothing else?

Gate fever. That was what they called it when prisoners had been locked up for so long they feared the outside world. Caron had watched a video about it once and thought yes, I can be like that. I can spend too much time in my own company that I think I'm happier that way. But in the end I never am, because I'm a prisoner of my past, and the only way to escape that is to get out and change my life.

So maybe the answer was to destroy Blaze's sense that the cage was a safe place. That seemed cruel, but as the saying went, sometimes you had to be cruel to be kind. Someone in Hamlet said that – it was the only line Caron could remember.

Caron crept round to the back of the cage, then gave it a sharp knock. Then another, and another. There seemed to be no response from Blaze, so she tried barking like a dog.

Still no response.

Caron crawled back round to the front of the cage. Blaze was now in a state of mortal terror, but no more inclined to move than ever. If it had an animal's instinct for fight or flight, it showed no sign of it. Any more of this tactic and Blaze would be traumatised for life.

"Oh come on, *please*. . ."

Caron's frustration was turning to desperation: her dreams of the fabulous time they would spend together were turning to ashes. Had she imagined this fantastic connection between them, was it just what she wanted to believe?

"You stupid, stupid. . ."

It was no good getting angry. That was another thing Blaze could not understand. Exhausted, Caron dropped down onto her side and gave in, stopped holding back the swell of emotions inside her. The tears came, just a trickle at first, then great heaving sobs. Yes, it was a relief, but it also made her feel weak, a feeling she hated, and a little sick.

Three, maybe four minutes passed, then, just as the sobs were beginning to subside, Caron felt something press against her arm.

Blaze?

Careful not to make any sudden movements, Caron gently turned her head. Yes! The little dragon was nestled against her, watching her with that same intensity she had noted the first time they had met. Was it responding to her distress? That seemed the only possible reason for its change of behaviour. It was something that cats sometimes did, and dogs: a necessary instinct for creatures who had babies to care for. Dragons didn't have babies, of course, and the exact way they had been created remained a secret, but it was likely that the genes of other creatures were involved.

Slowly, very slowly, Caron brought her other arm over and laid her hand against Blaze. Its scales were cool, surprisingly silky, softly swelling and contracting with each breath. However it had been created, it was alive now, responsive, aware of her in a way so many humans weren't.

Caron exhaled deeply. A new feeling of strength was filling her. It was as if her life so far had been a prologue, and now the story was finally beginning.

Sixteen

There was so much to learn about the dragon, and to Caron's delight, her curiosity was matched by Blaze's curiosity about its new home. There was not a corner that it did not want to explore: beneath the bed, inside the drawers, even that perfect dragon-sized bath whose water could be magically flushed away and refilled. How frustrating, however, that it could not simply fly up to such a thing as instinct demanded. Over and again it stretched out its wings, something it never could do in its cage, only to crash down on its side the moment it took off.

Caron did not know what to do about this. There was no point in encouraging it to keep trying: that withered wing would never function. But short of holding it down, what could she do? It had to learn its own way.

At least its claws worked, all too well in fact, since it clearly had the urge to dig, and turn a pile of Caron's old drawings into shredded paper in next to no time. Needless to say this did not please Caron, but it did give her an idea. How about if she drew Blaze? She had not touched a stick of charcoal since arguing with her art teacher, but suddenly the urge was back. This magic time, living with the dragon, was limited, but she could make something permanent from it, something the whole world could witness.

Not yet though. Caron knew how obsessive she became once she began to draw, and there were people she needed to contact before becoming a recluse: friends who lived at the lower end of town and whose homes were now underwater. Caron needed to know they were safe, and they needed to know about her as well. It was Caron's nature to share her feelings freely with people she trusted - but she would say nothing about Blaze. The experiences of the past week had left their mark.

Should she call Elf? No, she could not bring herself to do it.

Still, it was good to catch up with people. Caron was beginning to feel like her old self again, laughing and bantering, having the mickey taken out of her and giving as good as she got. After her round of calls she felt full of energy and could think of nothing better to do than put on some music and dance. This seemed to entrance Blaze: it stood stock still as she sashayed round the room, but its eyes were alive to every movement. Was it those movements that fascinated it, or her mood? It had responded to her distress – was it possible it also responded to her happiness? In which case, might it respond to all her moods?

Time would tell, but one thing was for certain: since coming out of the cage, Blaze was twice as confident and ten times as alive. Its coat even seemed brighter.

Science had never been Caron's favourite subject at school, but the urge to discover more about Blaze was inspiring her to devise all kinds of experiments. Everyone assumed that dragons ate nothing but Firefuel, eggsticks and, if they were lucky enough, the occasional live rodent, but how did they know? Why not test out the contents of the fridge and food cupboard on Blaze?

It wouldn't take that long. Having no-one else to look after, Caron pretty much lived from hand to mouth. But she did have some cheese – of no interest to Blaze – and some bean sprouts, which the little dragon found positively repugnant. It did have a sniff of some tinned spaghetti, before rejecting it, and was quite curious about a satsuma, but mainly as an item of play.

Then Caron opened the biscuit tin: the last four and a half custard creams were inside. Instant interest from Blaze. She took one out and held it close to the dragon's face: it was like holding a piece of raw liver close to a cat. Except Blaze was not a family pet, trained to wait for the pay-off moment. It seized the biscuit in its jaws, almost taking Caron's fingers with it, then guzzled it down with a relish that was quite scary. Not wanting to repeat the dangerous experience, Caron tipped the rest of the custard creams onto the floor and watched Blaze devour them like a top-of-the-range vacuum before looking round hungrily for more. When these weren't forthcoming, Blaze set off on another round of attempts to fly, all ending in undignified crashes.

Thankfully, in time, Blaze settled down again and began searching for a place to rest. Caron placed cushions on the floor for this purpose, but Blaze was more interested in her small sofa. After it had made a few hapless attempts to get up to this, Caron created a little staircase of books and shoe boxes, which Blaze successfully climbed. Now the little dragon felt happy and safe, curled up and for the first time since its arrival in the flat, closed its eyes.

Caron seized the moment. Out came her old easel, her cartridge pad, her charcoal. She set up quickly and hungrily, selected a willow vine stick and began work on the outline. Yes, she was in the zone, concentrating fiercely, determined to be accurate. To draw well, first you had to see well, and to see well you had to feel for your subject. That was easy when the subject was Blaze.

How wonderful it seemed, trying so hard to be true. Caron had become so used to a life of selling that she had forgotten what that felt like. Suddenly it seemed so strange to think of her time in the shop, all day saying things she didn't believe to persuade strangers to buy things they probably didn't need. And everyone else doing the same, their lives depending on it. No wonder society was in such a mess.

That withered wing was going to be difficult. Not just in terms of the outline: emotionally as well, as it brought her so close to the reality of Blaze's disability.

Leave it for now. Start working on the shading. Caron had always enjoyed this, getting her fingers dirty, smudging and blending. By now her confidence was growing and her concentration total: half an hour passed, then an hour. Still the little dragon slept.

Some areas were still not quite right. The tail was weak, the feet too small. But just as Caron was adjusting these, Blaze's eyes opened. His neck stretched forward and he began to cough.

"Blaze? Are you all right?"

Blaze was clearly not all right. The cough became more profound and a look of extreme distress overcame the dragon. Caron was seized by panic: she knew nothing of the diseases dragons might suffer from, or whether Blaze had some major internal problem. God, could it even be dying?

The answer came soon enough. A great convulsion went through the dragon's body, and out of its mouth, all over Caron's beloved sofa, came a gush of yellow slurry.

Caron had learnt an important lesson. Blaze, like a human child, ate what it liked the taste of, whether or not it was good for it.

Seventeen |

SEVENTEEN

It was 3 a.m. when the doorbell rang. First once, then again, then repeatedly for the next five minutes. This did happen from time to time: the porch with the doorbells was open to anybody, including drunk people ringing the wrong flat, or bored kids causing trouble. But if Caron ignored it she could be kept awake all night. Reluctantly, she pulled on a wraparound, put a hammer in her pocket and went down to the main hallway.

The visitor was still pressing the doorbell. Caron could make out a vague shape on the other side of the glass. Whoever it was did not look that big.

Ready for anything, Caron opened the front door.

"You took your time," said a familiar voice.

"If I'd known it was you I would've stayed in bed," replied Caron.

"Can I come in?"

"I suppose so."

Even after their great falling out Caron found it hard to say no to Elf. He had such an open, likeable face, no matter what nonsense sometimes came out of it. And he was clearly in a desperate state, like a half-drowned dog. Under the bright hallway light she could see his normally bright eyes stupefied by tiredness.

"I thought you were probably dead," she said.

"I probably am," he replied.

They went upstairs, but at the door of her flat, Caron paused.

"Just to let you know," she said, "there's a dragon in here, and it's not used to strangers."

"You're kidding."

"I am not."

"Does it bite?"

"I can't guarantee what it'll do."

"Ok. I like living dangerously."

It crossed Caron's mind to say that Elf's love of danger did not extend to him staying in his flooded home, but this was not the time to reopen that argument. They went into the flat, but this time Caron was not embarrassed that it was untidy, or worried about what was on the walls. Although she had not seen Elf for months, the old feeling had come back immediately: with him she did not feel like an outsider. With him she felt normal.

"Do you want a cup of something?" she asked.

"No thanks. Where's the dragon?"

"No, I want to know why you're here."

"Nowhere else to go."

"Well that's honest."

"Plan went wrong."

"What plan?"

"Chil's plan."

"Chilton? You were taking advice off Chilton?"

Chilton, to put it mildly, was an eccentric. Most people thought he was mentally ill. He just did not abide by normal standards of behaviour, right down to his habit of climbing lampposts or playing his penny whistle on buses. Elf enjoyed his company and generally looked after him, but the idea that he would depend on him in a crisis was bizarre.

"Chil knew this empty house in St Davids Square."

"What, you were going to burgle it?"

"It's called squatting."

"But you were going to break in?"

"Is that such a crime? When people are homeless and other people keep houses empty for profit?"

"I'm not saying it's wrong, I'm just saying you were asking for trouble."

"Yeah, well, Chil had stayed there before, except they'd obviously improved the alarms since then."

"Hardly surprising."

"Anyway, we couldn't get in, and I couldn't go anywhere else, not with Chil."

"Because no-one would have him."

"Would you?"

"No."

"Yeah, well that's why we ended up sleeping in a doorway."

"Oh god, I've been there. Did you actually sleep?"

"Not the first night. I must have dozed off tonight though, cos when I opened my eyes Chil had gone."

"No idea where?"

"Not a clue."

"Hasn't he got a phone?"

"Dead. Can I see the dragon now?"

"Elf, I've got to get back to sleep."

"God, you've changed."

"How do you mean?"

"What happened to the party girl?"

"I've got a job now."

"Have you got to get up tomorrow?"

"No."

"Then let's see this dragon!"

"Ok. But don't do anything to scare it. And once you've seen it, don't do anything to keep me awake."

By now Blaze had abandoned its favourite spot on the sofa. Maybe, like a cat, it had the instinct to keep changing its sleeping place, and also the instinct to climb into boxes, or half-opened drawers, one of which it had now turned into a makeshift nest. Elf gazed in wonderment at the sleeping creature, the corners of his mouth curling with delight.

"Wow," he said.

"It's got a withered wing," replied Caron. "That's why no-one's bought it."

Elf shrugged. He wasn't bothered by a withered wing.

"What a cool little dude," he said.

As if in reply, Blaze opened one eye. If it was bothered by the stranger now watching, it didn't show it. Instead it cocked its head upwards and regarded Elf with the same curious interest it had first shown Caron. Somehow it knew, as Caron had instantly known all those years ago, that Elf was an ally.

"Can we get it out?" asked Elf.

"Elf," replied Caron, "you need to sleep."

It wasn't unusual for Caron to adopt a motherly tone with Elf. Let's face it, he needed it. He had all the enthusiasm of a five-year-old, and as much commonsense.

"Just for five minutes," said Elf.

Not wanting to be pestered for the rest of the night, Caron agreed. She lifted Blaze out of its cosy corner and the moment it was down on the carpet, Elf was down there with it, pulling a lace from his boot and drawing it enticingly along the ground for its eyes to follow. Yes, it was up for play, and the rapport between the two grew rapidly. Despite herself, Caron could not help feeling a twinge of jealousy.

"Have you played it any music?" asked Elf.

"Yes, I've done that."

"How did it react?"

"It seemed to like it. Although I was dancing. It might have just liked me dancing."

"Have you still got that little keyboard?"

"Elf, not now."

"I want to get it to run over the keys, see how it reacts to that."

“You said five minutes. Five minutes is up. Elf, I need to sleep!”

“Whatever you say, party girl.”

Eighteen

Caron was woken next morning by a familiar smell, but one from long ago. It was the smell of a fried breakfast, and sure enough that breakfast was soon presented to her, on a makeshift tray, by a grinning Elf.

"Eggs on toast," she said delighted. "Elf, that's really sweet of you."

"One night's rent," replied Elf.

Caron hooked Elf in with her free arm and gave him half a hug. It felt good, like the times she used to hug her dad, before he'd done so much damage she didn't want to touch him anymore.

"Hang on," she said. "Where did you get the eggs? I don't have any eggs."

"Your neighbour."

"What, the old guy?"

"That's him. Matt."

"Is that his name?"

"What, haven't you ever spoken to him?"

"I say hello, but he doesn't seem to want to talk. I think he's scared of me."

"I think he's scared of me too. That's why he gave me the eggs."

It was so typical of Elf. He was a boy who could have got away with murder. That was why it had been so hard to fall out with him, because everyone knew him, everyone liked him, and no-one was likely to take her side.

Caron tucked into the breakfast. How amazing it seemed, someone doing something nice for her, not expecting her to do a day's work before getting any kind of reward. And how wonderful to look forward to the day ahead, a day of playing with Blaze and catching up with Elf's adventures. She had no idea what he'd been up to, but she could be sure he'd have stories to tell.

And so he did. He'd come across an empty warehouse and was creating a whole sound-and-visual experience there, along with a few friends, some of which Caron had never heard of. It sounded so exciting. But for Elf, nothing at that moment was more exciting than the little dragon. They did find the keyboard, and set Blaze loose on it, although the music it accidentally made did not seem to mean much to it. It was much more interested in what was outside the window, or inside the few nooks and crannies it had not yet explored. How ridiculous it was to call this creature second quality! Those lumbering beasts up at Ruby Street might be able to breathe fire, but other than that, what were they? Hardly better than vegetables, sitting inert in their fancy cages with barely the initiative to turn their heads! Blaze might be small and have a withered wing, but other than that, it was superior in every way!

The hours eased past as Caron and Elf took it in turns to find new experiences for Blaze: the chemistry between them was the same as ever, both happy to sometimes lead, sometimes follow. How different that was to the world of work, where the same person was boss every day. It surely wasn't beyond the wit of human beings to create a better way.

Outside, however, the waters were beginning to recede.

"I'm dreading going back to work," Caron said.

"Then don't," replied Elf.

"No choice."

"There's always a choice."

"Not if I want a home and an income."

"I manage."

"You've just been sleeping on the street!"

"Come on, Caz, why don't you do a runner? I'll go with you. And you'll have Blaze!"

"Doing what?"

"We'll work the festivals. There's always jobs there if you know where to go."

"I'm not living in a tent."

"A motorhome. Or a boat even."

"I don't have a motorhome or a boat."

"You can get them for next to nothing."

Elf's enthusiasm was infectious. Was it true what he'd been saying, that she'd got too stuck in her ways? Had she lost her sense of adventure? But then she knew too many people who lived the way he talked about, and weren't they all running away from something? Caron did not want to be someone who ran away. She could never forget what she'd seen at Sky-larks.

Caron had not yet mentioned the dragon fights to Elf, but the urge to tell him was now irresistible. Out it all came, and in his company, her full emotions overtook her. She began to cry, uncontrollably; Elf shyly put a hand upon her shaking shoulder.

"I've tried to get it stopped," she said, "but no-one seems to want to know."

"Typical," said Elf.

"Will you help me?" pleaded Caron. She had not intended to ask this, but all her defences were down.

Elf was strangely quiet.

"You know so many people," added Caron.

Elf still said nothing.

"Well?" said Caron.

"It's difficult."

"In what way?"

"I mean, yeah, it's bad. But that don't mean we've got the right to stop them doing it, does it?"

"Why not?"

"I don't want to be a hypocrite, Caz. A lot of people don't like what I do."

"Yeah, but you're not killing dragons!"

"But you can't say, I want my freedom, but you can't have yours."

"No-one should have the freedom to do what they're doing!"

"See, that's where we differ, Caz."

Was this a wind-up? Suddenly they were back to square one, where Caron no longer knew whether Elf was joking or serious. And maybe he didn't know either. Maybe, like so many people she knew, his mind was like a warzone between opposing armies. And dealing with him would leave her exhausted.

"I didn't like that song you wrote about me by the way," she said.

"What song?"

"Oh come on, you know it was about me."

"You might be a bit paranoid, Caron."

"So everyone tells me."

"Sorry I don't agree with you about everything."

"That's alright. I think you'd better go now."

"Ok."

Caron watched Elf pack his things, wondering if this time the break might be final.

Nineteen

Dav rang the next day. The authorities had given the all-clear and the shop was reopening in the morning. Dav would arrive at Caron's flat at eight o'clock sharp to pick up Blaze.

This would have to take some preparing for. Caron had not been outside of her flat, even into the hallway, since Blaze had arrived. Just to go out onto the street seemed a daunting task. Several times she had been on the point of visiting the local shop, if this was open, to get some eggs for her neighbour, but had always found a reason to stay put. Now, however, it was vital she rejoined the big wide world.

It wasn't easy to leave Blaze. It felt wrong. How Caron would have loved to take the dragon with her, trotting alongside her. Not on a lead – that would be unthinkable – just there by its own free will. People would get used to seeing them together, and call Caron the Dragon Girl, an identity she would be comfortable with. For once in her life, she would feel complete.

But that was all idle fantasy. They would have to part, at least for twenty minutes. Caron made sure Blaze had food, something to play with, and a reassuring farewell message.

"I won't be long little one," she said, hoping that if she spoke with enough emphasis, and looked into the dragon's eyes, it would somehow understand.

Then out, quickly, no looking back.

The streets were quiet, but other than that, nothing much had changed. How strange it was to think of the utter chaos that must have existed less than a mile away in the low-lying parts of town. It was easy to see how rich people could be so oblivious to the fate of the poor.

Caron had mixed feelings when she saw Janine at the Co-op. The friendliest of the checkout operators, she always exchanged a few words with Caron, and Caron generally being an open person usually gave as good as she got. But things were different now. She didn't want Janine to know anything about what she'd been up to since the flood, since she'd probably tell the next customer and the one after that, and you never knew who that might be. So she claimed to be in a hurry, and as she departed the shop with eggs and bread, her steps did indeed speed up. It really had not been good to leave Blaze alone.

No time to talk to the neighbour. Caron left the eggs by the door, knocked it, then hastened to her own door, which she opened cautiously, ready to block the way should Blaze make a sudden bolt for freedom.

No need. No sign of the little dragon. All was quiet, disturbingly so.

Caron checked Blaze's favourite haunts: beneath the bed, inside the wardrobe, among the piles of clothes left untidily around the bedroom. No dragon to be seen.

Suddenly the conversations in the Brazil Café came back to Caron. Farah knew where she lived. And who knew what went on in Farah's mind? Did she have a key? Jak Dekker had a key, of course, and how about Bryn, the handyman? Nothing would surprise Caron about him. Hell, why had she risked leaving Blaze alone?

Now in a flat panic, Caron redoubled her efforts to find the dragon: opening every drawer, opening and reopening every cupboard door, throwing her dirty clothes out of the laundry basket. But it was only when she checked under the sofa for the third time that she made a disturbing discovery. The sash window above the sofa, which she'd opened a crack to air the room that morning, was still open. Open far enough for a small dragon to squeeze through.

Caron seized the bottom rail of the window, hauled it open and thrust her head out. It was impossible to see down to the ground because of an overhanging ledge the floor below. But the drop was at least four metres. No animal could survive that fall, even a cat. But then, no animal would be stupid enough to try – unless it thought it could fly.

What an idiot she was! She should never, never, never have tried to take responsibility for another living thing! Now she would have to live with the consequences, not just that day, or that week, but for the rest of her life!

In a haze of unreality, Caron tore down the stairway from her flat, out into the side yard, prepared for the sight of Blaze's still and broken body. But there was nothing to be found. Had someone found it and buried it? Thrown it in a bin? Had the rats had it, or the crows?

Caron wandered aimlessly around the perimeter of the building, as if Blaze could have somehow dragged its shattered body to a dark corner somewhere, but it was a fruitless search, and eventually she re-entered the stairwell and trudged back upstairs to her flat. It was impossible to know what to do: she was in a state of shock. Her body was telling her to vomit.

Caron went to the kitchen sink. The kitchen was her least favourite part of the flat, cramped, unwelcoming, with an ancient washing machine, a tumble drier she rarely used, a boiler which regularly broke down and water pipes that creaked and rattled. As she leaned over the sink, however, her ears detected a new noise: a scratching.

Caron investigated the noise: no, not mice under the sink again. It came from the washing machine – or was it the tumble drier?

Good God, there was something inside there!

Caron pulled open the door.

Blaze!

A thankful dragon clambered out and was clasped in an embrace of utter relief. However had it got into there? Had she left the door open then closed it with the creature inside? Hell, what if she'd thrown clothes inside and turned it on?

But she hadn't. Thank God she hadn't and thank God Blaze was alive. Never, never would she let it out of her sight again!

Suddenly Caron knew, with total certainty, that she could not accept Blaze going back on sale the next day.

Twenty

The dragon which for so long had refused to leave its cage was now twice as reluctant to re-enter it. How Caron longed to be able to explain what was happening, make it understand it was all for the best, but there was no way. In the end she had no alternative but to tempt it close to the cage door, then use physical force to drive it inside. Had that destroyed the trust she had so carefully built? Only time would tell. But right now, time was short: Dav was waiting.

"How's Puff the Magic Dragon?" was his opening shot.

"Good," replied Caron.

"Just as well. Clapton's not coming till Friday. Your dragon's all we've got."

They set off, back down the hill, where the residue of the flood was soon apparent. Sandbags were still out, signs down, wrecked cars lying where they were deposited, and a grim tide-mark evident along the rows of terrace houses.

Caron plucked up the courage to say what she had resolved to say from the moment she found Blaze in the tumble drier.

"I want to buy the dragon," she said

Dav gave a little laugh. "You're so predictable, Caz," he replied.

"In what way?" snapped Caron. The idea that Dav could read her was beyond annoying.

"I should have warned you not to get involved with the thing."

Caron's irritation grew. "What's it to you?" she said. "My money's as good as anyone else's."

"There's no staff discount."

"I didn't think there was."

"Caz, why don't you wait till Friday? You can get a new one, without the wonky wing."

"I want this one."

"Oh dear. I guess it's something to do with the mothering instinct."

"I haven't got a bloody mothering instinct. I just like this dragon, ok?"

"Okay, cut the swearing. If you want it you can have it. But not till Friday."

"Why not?"

"I told you, it's the only dragon we've got. We need to put it in the window to show we're back in business."

"But it doesn't want to be in a cage anymore."

"That's the deal. Take it or leave it."

Caron knew she had no choice but was far from happy. Blaze, in the window? That would not be a good experience, on show to the world, people pointing and laughing, lights, noise, traffic. . .

Reluctantly she agreed, Blaze's cage was placed in the window, vans arrived with the converters and other sundries, and

Caron joined the others in restoring the shop to something like normality. But nothing really was normal anymore. Jac Dekker had installed a noisy temporary generator as none of the electrics were safe, along with heavy duty fans to dry everything out, while an engineer was on hand to check for structural damage, and a small army of van boys and Temps shovelled silt into piles which Bryn the handyman removed with a wheelbarrow. The shop had become a morbid shadow of its old self, infused with a stench of damp and dirt. It was a place where Caron no longer wanted to be.

Fortunately the creatures in the second-hand warehouse had survived. Whether the experience had affected them was hard to judge since most were in such a dire state already, but Caron renewed their food and water. Going across the road then back to the shop was her only opportunity to see Blaze, since the old-fashioned bay window could only be accessed by a key, and the only people who had one were Dav and Farah, who was nowhere to be seen. Caron noted that Blaze had not settled back to cage life and was biting at the bars, something it had never done before. She so wished she could tell the little dragon that freedom was just a couple of days away.

A few customers did wander in through the day. Caron had wondered if the flood would have caused everyone to seek converters or dragon food online, but of course, as well as the shops being closed, deliveries had been impossible to this end of town. So Caron had to deal with them, give them the usual patter, but could not disguise her lack of enthusiasm. Then, just as she was gratefully noting there were just twenty more minutes to survive, she heard voices that threw her head into chaos.

Batman and Robin.

Caron hurried into the tearoom. If she had despised the pair before, it was nothing to what she felt now. What, was she supposed to speak to them politely, smile at their pathetic jokes, let them patronise her like she was five years old?

It wasn't going to happen.

"Caz!" yelled Dav.

"In the toilet!"

"Good god, do you live in there?"

A much-displeased Dav stomped down the shop to deal with the pair himself.

Caron opened the door a crack.

"Gentlemen!" began Dav. "What can I do you for today?"

"Alright, butt?" said Batman. "Where's the dragons?"

"They're in Friday"

"That's no good to us, pal."

"Bamps got flooded out," added Robin. "Lost everything."

"Sorry to hear that," said Dav. "I'll reserve one for you if you like."

"What about the one in the window?" asked Batman.

Caron's heart began to thump.

"Sorry gents, that's just for display."

"How much do you want for it? We'll pay it."

"It is second quality, guys. It's not like the others."

"What's wrong with it?"

"Withered wing."

"Can it walk?"

"It can walk, but – "

"Let's have a look at it."

There was a pause.

"If you insist," said Dav. He located the key to the window display, unlocked it and admitted Batman and Robin. Seconds later he was face to face with a red-faced Caron.

"You're not letting them buy it!" she said.

"Don't you start," he replied.

"You promised it to me!"

"They're our best customers."

"They're murderers!"

"Keep your voice down."

"I don't care if they hear."

"Well I do."

"We don't have to sell it to them! We're not legally obliged to sell anything to anybody!"

"I know the law, thank you."

"We're not selling them that dragon!"

 "Who's the manager here?"

Caron could not hide her contempt. "You're no better than they are!" she raged.

Dav's face hardened. "You'd better get your coat," he said.

It was just how school had ended, and once again, there was no rowing back.

"Ok," Caron replied. Oblivious to the consequences, she marched back to the tearoom, at the door of which stood Dobbin, who did nothing to hide the delight on his face.

"Take a picture, it lasts longer," said Caron, pushing past him into the room and slamming the door behind her. She cursed herself for not thinking of a more original put-down, but her street wisdom had deserted her. For a few moments her eyes fell on Dobbin's coat, and Dav's, but no, she would not sink to their level again. But if she was really being sacked, what was to stop her confronting Batman and Robin?

Caron stood motionless in the centre of that dingy little room, breathing deeply, rehearsing the scene. For all her instinctive bravery, she could not deny they scared her. But the thought of Blaze in that hellish pit scared her more.

Could she? Could she? What could she say? How could she stop them?

Caron's hesitation was fatal. When she finally stormed back into the shop, prepared for confrontation, Batman and Robin had gone. And so had Blaze.

Twenty One

Caron was twelve when she had her first fight. There had been confrontations before, plenty of them, but not like this. Selma Pugh was a hard case, only remaining daughter of a mother who'd had all her other children taken by the authorities. She had a phone at the age of seven, was vaping by ten, and had caused innumerable suffering to the many girls, and a few boys, she bullied. Caron had made a comment about her online, never suspecting she'd get to hear about it, but like every bully she had a network of informers keen to suck up to her. So one day, as Caron was quietly eating lunch in the school canteen, Selma arrived with a little gang bent on confrontation. Caron was a coward, she said, saying online what she would never dare say to Selma's face. Selma wanted satisfaction. That meant a fight.

Caron was very scared. In anger Selma seemed so like her father in one of his violent tempers. In the face of those rages, despite the defiant face she put on, Caron was never anything but a helpless victim. But if she backed out of the fight with Selma the whole school would know.

Three hours of pure adrenaline followed. Selma wasn't big, but when she fought she was ruthlessly efficient and equally vicious. Caron faced the possibility of being hurt badly. Made to grovel, made to cry, her humiliation watched by every person she had wanted to impress. So, she made a decision. She would convert all the fear she felt into a tide of aggression so shocking that Selma's confidence would evaporate.

It worked. No-one who witnessed it would ever forget the absolute insanity of her performance: the banshee cries, the whirling arms, the sheer unstoppable manic energy. No-one at that school would ever challenge her again.

But she was not facing a twelve-year-old girl now. To save Blaze she would have to confront grown men for whom violence was a way of life. Caron had no illusions about the danger she was putting herself in, but so what? She had no choice.

Strangely, Caron had never thought more clearly. Before she had even got home she had engaged a locksmith, and half an hour later he was unscrewing the faceplate at the edge of the door, removing the lock and replacing it with a new one. That would be a nice surprise for Jak Dekker's handymen, coming to remove her belongings and finding the lock was already changed and they couldn't get in.

There was no doubt in Caron's mind that the dragon fights would be taking place that night. The last time Batman and Robin bought a dragon, there had been no delay in using it. No longer afraid of her messages being intercepted, she notified every group she belonged to about what would be happening at Skylarks that night. But she did not assume that anyone would respond.

Before the same mirror that had watched her prepare for her day in Ruby Street, Caron selected a pair of jeans, a dark top with hood and a pair of walking boots. Should she take a weapon? That would raise the stakes. She hadn't needed a weapon when she fought Selma Pugh.

Caron opened the top drawer of her dresser and took out a can of self-defence spray. She had never used it and could not be sure it even worked. But according to the instructions it had a range of four metres and would startle and confuse an attacker. She put the spray in her bag, picked up her helmet, gave a final reassurance to her own reflection, and walked out into the fading light.

Could Caron rely on her old delivery scooter? It was hardly the ideal getaway vehicle. But it was what she knew, which gave her some comfort. She climbed aboard, switched on the engine, and set off with a grim determination. At fist the route seemed familiar, but as she descended onto the coast road she entered a world utterly changed, dreamlike: so much broken wood, mainly cleared to either side, but still the cabin of a small boat straddling the white lines, a car upturned, and everywhere hordes of screaming gulls fighting over stranded crabs. What state would Skylarks be in, she wondered? Would the pool be full of water and unusable? If so, why did the dynamic duo so desperately need a dragon?

Feverish thoughts began racing helter-skelter through Caron's head. A coastal road is called a corniche. Seawater is thirty-five per cent salt. The suffragette killed by the king's horse did not intend to die. How did you empty a swimming pool, was there a plughole, like in a bath?

So many brave people had died at the hands of evil ones.

What parent would not die for the life of their child?

Why has that van not overtaken me?

Caron glanced in her rear-view mirror. The van had been behind her for at least a mile. She could just make out a dark shape at the wheel. Was she being followed?

Caron slowed down. The van slowed. Yes, she was being followed.

Caron sped up.

The van sped up.

Clearly the driver knew who Caron was, and possibly where she was going. That was some bad luck, messaging all her friends and only attracting an enemy. An enemy who had presumably been tracking her since she left the flat.

What could she do? She couldn't outrun the van. There were no side roads to take, nowhere else to go except off the road and into the trees, dangerous and futile since she could never get to Skylarks that way.

She could, however, stop. If she stopped and the van stopped also, it would be obvious it was following her. Would the driver be prepared to show their hand?

Caron stopped.

The van stopped.

Caron climbed off the scooter. Preparing herself as well as she could, she began walking back towards the van. *Be aggressive*, she told herself. *Just like when you fought Selma.*

There was no move from the driver. The windows were tinted and it was impossible to tell who or what was sitting there.

So what now?

Start the way you mean to go on. Confront them.

Caron rapped on the door.

The window wound down.

"Hello Caron."

Good god. Farah!

Smiling, like she'd just met Caron for a night out!

"What are you doing?" said Caron, meeting Farah's smile with a furious glare.

"Are you going to Skylarks?" replied Farah.

There was no point in denying it.

"How do you know that?" she demanded.

"Caron," she replied, "there's a tag in your bag."

"*What?*" Caron began rummaging furiously in her bag. "How long has that been there?"

Suddenly the memory of Dobbin returned. So that was what he was doing! And people called her paranoid?

Caron found the tag, but before she could dash it on the pavement, Farah advised her to keep it. "It's better I can keep track on you," she said.

"Why should I want you to do that?"

"Because I'm on your side."

"Like hell you are."

"Come and sit up here a second."

"I haven't got a second."

Farah consulted her phone. "You've got fifty-five minutes," she said.

Caron was stunned. "You know about the dragon fights?" she said.

"Yes."

Caron stared at Farah, aghast. "Then why haven't you done anything about it?"

"Sit up here. We need to talk."

Caron walked round the van and climbed into the passenger seat. But sitting next to Farah only made her feel more hostile and suspicious.

"Does this van come with the job?" she asked, pointedly.

"What if it does?"

"Done well out of the old man, haven't you? No wonder you admire him."

"Caron, that's all an act."

"So how do I know you're not acting now?"

"Caron, I needed to suss you out."

"Yeah, to check my loyalty."

"No, to check how you felt about the dragons."

"Why?"

"Ok, Caron, I can tell you this now because I trust you, right? I'm not what I seem to be, Caron. I'm not loyal to Jac Dekker, and I'm not naïve. I'm working in the dragon business in order to destroy it."

Caron's mind immediately summoned up the image of her friend Bel, the day she discovered she'd been living with an undercover police agent. Bel was devastated. She had never really recovered.

"Are you saying you're the police?" she asked.

"God no," said Farah.

"Then what are you?"

"I can't tell you."

"Then I can't believe you."

"All you need to know is, I'm against the FB."

"Who's the FB?"

"Seriously?"

"I've never heard of the FB."

"The Freedom Boys. The people who run the dragon fights."

"It's just a couple of guys who come in the shop."

"It's more organised than that Caron."

Caron viewed Farah long and hard. She was so used to Farah's chatty, slightly dim manner that she had never noticed the flinty determination of her eyes.

But to trust her? To trust anybody now?

"So you're in with other people?" she asked.

"Yes. We all work on the inside. We figure that the more important we are to the dragon trade, the easier it will be to end it."

"So you're living a lie."

"The end justifies the means."

"Don't ask me to do it."

"I'm not."

"So how are you going to help me?"

"By giving you advice."

"Such as?"

"Don't do this tonight."

It was the last thing Caron wanted to hear.

"I have to," she replied.

"You need to play the long game, Caz."

"No, I need to save my dragon! Don't you understand? They've got my dragon!"

The force of Caron's emotion silenced Farah for a moment.

"Sorry, I didn't realise you had a dragon," she said.

"It was promised to me! But Dav just went and sold it to them!"

"But what can you do, Caron?"

"Just shut up! Shut up negging me! Unlike you, I *am* going to do something!"

Caron threw open the van door, leapt out, and marched back to her scooter. All Farah had managed to do was break her concentration and throw her head into turmoil. Tears were welling up, the same tears she had fought back that time her dad had lined her up alongside her sisters and brother, then made them bend over while he took off his gym shoe and leathered each one of them, not in temper this time, just to show his mastery. Even Carl cried out, but not Caron. Her teeth were grit so tight she cracked the enamel on two of them, but not one tiny cry escaped her lips.

Nor would she show weakness now.

Twenty Two

It was as if the planet was already finished. Besides the sad ruins of the chalets and playgrounds of the Skylarks Holiday Park lay every piece of detritus that humanity had consigned to the ocean: plastic bottles, tin cans, rubber tyres, wooden pallets, circuit boards, used nappies, shirts, socks, shoes. And into this dismal wasteland the living dead were fast assembling, seemingly blind to its squalor, as if they were in an invisible tunnel, totally focussed on the gory spectacle at the end of it.

The smell was awful: an all-pervading perfume of death and decay. It reminded Caron when she'd first had a bad tooth, and the dentist's drill had released the foul odour of pus. But this was a hundred times worse.

Somewhere up ahead, Blaze was going through its own private hell. Had they fed it, or did they think a hungry dragon would make a better fight? Was it terrified, did it have any sense of what it was about to face? Or wonder why Caron had abandoned it?

Such thoughts were like spurs in Caron's sides, pain erasing doubt as she made her way between the mass of cars and vans to join the crocodile of fight fans. No-one would single her out because of her clothing, as almost everybody was partly hidden by hoods, caps and helmets, but no-one else was pushing a vehicle – if all went well, her getaway vehicle, with its dragon-sized pizza delivery box.

So many people. More than last time. Maybe the days hiding from the flood had sharpened their appetite for their chosen sport. Yes, sport, that's how they saw it, like the rich people who still chased foxes. And to think there was talk that the flood was some kind of divine judgement on human sin. If so, why weren't all these people dead, instead of the random assortment of children, old people, mothers, fathers?

Over and again Caron rehearsed the plan in her head. Could she really rely on the self-defence spray to clear her exit? Why hadn't she read the reviews – not the five-star ones which were almost certainly placed by the manufacturers, or the one-star ones placed by their competitors, but the two- or three-star ones which might actually be genuine? Could she really believe what it said on the can? Caron knew all about sales patter: she spent every day selling things that didn't do what they were supposed to.

The old pool loomed closer, more ominous than ever. Had she made a massive mistake, not even asking Farah to help her? Might not the crowd think twice about attacking a disabled person? Or were they so devoid of feeling that they would have no hesitation? Yes, and in that situation, wouldn't Farah have made things more difficult?

Caron would never know the answers to these questions. She was on her own and edging towards the doors.

Caron thought back again to her fight with Selma, the fear she'd felt then and the mania she had turned it into. But into her mind came another memory: the school play for which she had auditioned, then, to her surprise, landed a major part in. For weeks she had lain awake going over her lines, desperate not to make a fool of herself. And then the opening night, hearing her name called by the stage manager, finding herself paralysed, terrified, understanding for the first time what was meant by stage fright. Nothing could make her go out before that audience. So she ran, out of the school hall, through the school gates, past the shops, the car showrooms, the medical centre, all the way home. It was a failure so awful she had blocked it from her mind.

Till now.

Caron parked her scooter. She realised her hands were shaking uncontrollably.

The pool was already full, but people were not silent as before. There was a steady hubbub from the crowd, a simmering undercurrent of violence, as if they were spurred on by the sea's brutality: every window had been smashed and hastily swept mounds of broken glass lay around the silt-covered floor. Almost nothing remained now of the old lockers or any other evidence that this had once been a place of joy. The smell was acrid with sweat, the air bitingly cold, and every face, no matter its form, impossibly ugly. It was an ugliness which derived from ugly intentions, and this time Caron knew exactly what these were, just as she knew the order of proceedings, what would be brought into that sinister arena and what would happen if she did not act.

Other things had changed. Behind the decks was a giant New Union flag, and the music which now broke out was no longer random top fifty hits, but AI-beat versions of old patriotic tunes. These brought about a waving of other flags from the audience, flags Caron had never seen before, most with the initials FB emblazoned. But the odd thing was, many of these Freedom Boys flags were waved by women. Caron wondered if her sister Elsie might be among them.

Maybe this would be Elsie's opportunity to kill her.

Or vice versa.

For a few moments Caron was transported back to her first festival. A sea of flags as far as the eye could see, and Caron could see a long way, up there on her dad's shoulders. Caron's dad was still enthusiastic for music in those days, before his own band had folded and his own hopes been crushed. That was when he started slagging off everything, including any music that she had taken to. It was also when the rows with her mum had started, rows which always ended with her apologising, no matter that it was invariably him in the wrong.

But forget that now. The music had stopped and someone was being introduced. He was obviously a big name to the crowd, judging by the reception he got. There he stood, in a velvet-collared suit, a luxury watch on his wrist, a self-satisfied look on his face. He took a long drag on a cigarette, then blew out smoke, which for some reason elicited a cheer. Then he began to speak, in that slow self-assured style of a man been to an expensive private school. He hoped everyone would enjoy tonight's entertainment. But there were bigger issues at stake. Their freedoms were under threat. The country was going to the dogs. It was time to make a stand.

Right on cue, others moved through the crowd, and Caron found a leaflet pushed into her hand. It read "Why YOU must join the Freedom Boys," followed by a web address, a picture of a bunch of triumphant looking knuckle-draggers and some more text which Caron did not bother to read. In any other situation she would have screwed up the leaflet and thrown it back at the person who'd handed it to her.

A word came to Caron, another taught her by Mr Cummins: *demagogue*. A demagogue was a person who used lies and misinformation to whip up anger, fear and hatred. And the man with the luxury watch was obviously a seasoned expert at this: the crowd were responding to his every provocation. His speech built towards its crescendo: soon, he said, their time would come: what they believed was what all ordinary people believed. It was time for men to be men again, and women to be women, and together, to take back the nation.

But right now. . .it was showtime.

Blood began beating in Caron's ears: a thudding like a temple drum. The crowd were beginning the countdown: big belly-shouts, raucous, inhuman. Floodlights lit up the old pool. And down the steps to the floor of this came four men, as before, carrying bulging hessian sacks.

Blaze. In there. Hefted around like rubbish.

Seconds out – round one!

There was a guttural roar as the first bag was emptied. Out dropped a fully functional, angry dragon: the victor of the last fight, gagging for more blood. The dragon's body whipped about like a salted slug, spurred by the noise, set for an enemy.

And now, from the second bag, Blaze tumbled to the floor in an undignified heap. Its unusable wing flailed hopelessly as the confused and frightened creature sought to upright itself.

The roars turned to laughter.

Caron's doubts and fears evaporated. All that existed now was a blind, unreasoning love. It was not a matter of choosing to protect the creature she loved, because no choice was involved. She could no more stand back than the morning sun could fail to rise. As the enemy dragon lurched threateningly towards Blaze, she was already on her way down the steps. Before the fight could begin she was between the two dragons.

"It's over, it's over!" she cried.

The hostility that Caron now faced was off the scale. The bag-carriers came for her without hesitation, but they were called back and displaced by a familiar figure: Batman.

Caron stood her ground as he prowled towards her. Her lifetime instinct kicked in: she showed no fear.

"Alright, love?" said Batman.

"Still want my phone number?" said Caron.

Batman laughed. "Past your bedtime, honey," he said.

"You wanted my phone number. Have you forgotten?"

Batman laughed again. "Get out."

Caron's hand crept towards the pocket where her defence spray was waiting.

Batman moved closer.

In a flash the spray was in Caron's hand.

"Are you threatening me?" raved Batman. "Are you threatening me?"

Caron pressed the nozzle. A weak jet of liquid escaped, just enough to leave a small red stain on Batman's t-shirt. Batman looked down in disgust, then whipped a dark object from his trouser pocket: a cosh, solid lead in a sheath of black leather. Caron had seen such a thing in the hands of bouncers. She knew that one blow from it could knock her unconscious. Enough force and it could kill her.

Batman's arm rose. Caron pressed again and again on the spray, but nothing came from it. Her father's angry face flashed across her mind. She raised a forearm in a desperate attempt to protect her head.

But no blow came.

Instead, a cry of agony.

The cosh dropped to the ground.

Batman clutched his hand. It was smoking.

So was Blaze's mouth.

Before Carons' astonished eyes, a jet of blue flame shot from the little dragon's mouth, again hitting Batman, again bringing out a howl of pain.

The crowd was now completely silent.

Next second, chaos.

Smoke bombs were going off all round the room. Figures were pouring through the door. Through the smoky haze Caron recognised the giant dreadlocked figure of Chilton, then more familiar faces, including the unmistakable curls of her greatest frenemy.

Seizing the chance, Caron ducked down and grabbed her beloved dragon, who, despite its terrified state, accepted her arms with total trust. She ran past her stricken enemy, still nursing his wounded hands, up the pool steps and through the confused and chaotic crowd. A few still attempted to bar her way, but these were soon scattered by the jets of blue flame spouting from Blaze's mouth.

The route to the doors was clear. Caron escaped the pool and mounted her scooter unopposed. With Blaze secure in the delivery box she headed back through the holiday park and out of the gates.

But Caron was far from safe. No matter what was happening at the pool, it was a sure thing that some of that vile crowd would get to their vehicles, and there was no way she would be able to outrun them: the scooter did 45 km/h at best. Of course, Caron had known this, and had planned to hide up among the pine trees that lay off to the right of the road, but she had made no more than a kilometre before headlights appeared behind her. If she came off the road her pursuers would see where she had gone.

Did Blaze have any fire left in it? There was no way to know. The most expensive dragons could pretty much produce at will, but the fact Blaze had produced at all was miraculous, and she feared it was already exhausted.

The lights were getting closer. Caron's eyes searched desperately for a way out. If she went for the trees would the scooter keep going, or get caught in the undergrowth? If she had an accident it could hurt Blaze and wreck any chances she had of escape.

If only there were a side turning! If only there was any alternative to this lonely coast road!

And what was this now? A van up ahead, not moving.

Wait – was that Farah's van?

Was Farah still there? Why?

There was only one explanation. Farah was blocking her way because all she had told Caron had been a pack of lies. Of course she had advised her not to go to Skylarks! She'd been a company spy from day one!

Well, she was not going to beat Caron that easily. Using every ounce of strength in her body, Caron swerved onto the grass verge, fighting to control the dangerously unstable scooter, jerking and bouncing over the rough terrain till she was past the van and back onto the road.

Caron checked her rear-view mirror. What? The van was turning, as if to go back the other way. Except then it stopped, sideways across the road. The van was now blocking the lanes either way, ignoring the honking horns and angry yells of the chasing pack. But there was nothing the pursuers could do. There they remained, stuck behind the roadblock, unable in any way to reach Caron.

The chase was over. Caron rode back to town in a flush of self-belief, her beloved dragon alive and secure, her elation only tempered by the fact that she had got a certain person very wrong.

Twenty Three ▌

Caron laid down her pencil and studied her drawing. The outline was pretty good, the eyes were in the right place, but no, she hadn't got the look in them, that spark of life which set Blaze apart. Not for the first time she wished she was Sofia, who she'd so often sat next to in art class. Sofia could look at anything and reproduce it in exact detail on paper. Then again Sofia was autistic. Would Caron choose to be neurodivergent if it meant drawing so perfectly? And would she want Blaze to be any different, to have both wings working, when its oddness was part of its charm, and maybe contributed to its unique personality?

Such questions were often in Caron's mind now that she not only looked after Blaze, but a range of young children. Not for one second had she dreamt of becoming a childminder, nor did she intend to do it for long, but it provided her with an income: part of the deal she'd made with Farah which included the flat she now lived in. It was hard work, harder than she'd expected, but no-one was bossing her around, and she got to meet some great parents, all part of the network of people fighting the dragon trade.

Now that fight was out in the open. Videos had been posted online, a big storm had been created in the media, motions had been passed at union conferences and even the prime minister had been forced to make a statement, defending the legality of the fights but raising some questions about dragon welfare. Laughable, according to Elf: it was wrong, everyone knew it was wrong, it had to be stopped. Ending the misuse of dragons had given him a purpose in life, and many others too.

Caron was part of that battle, but for now she was laying low: according to the law she was a thief and inevitably she was the target of vicious hatred. But on the flip side, she had won the respect of so many people, respect she had craved all her life, respect she was still denied by her family, who understood her as little as ever. To her dad, she had blown it again: a good job with prospects thrown away for the sake of a stupid animal. To her mum, she was still the same girl she was at twelve, in need of support and advice, which she received in the form of daily texts, deleted as soon as they appeared.

In fact, Carons' old job did not exist anymore. Sales had dwindled at Toadstool Lane and Jac Dekker had made the decision to carry on with just the Ruby Street store. Being a sound businessman, he knew that no matter how bad things got, the luxury market would never dry up.

Caron put her drawing aside. She would try again, but now she needed some play time. Barely a day went by without Blaze showing some new ability or awareness, and right now it was anxious to explore a shopping bag which Caron had left by its favourite sleeping place on the camp bed. Caron got down on hands and knees to share its experience, feeling, despite her perilous situation, a blissful peace of mind. Everything she felt inside was now on the outside.

An old song came to her lips:

"Ain't nothing like the real thing baby

Ain't nothing like the real thing. . ."

The real thing cocked its head and listened. People said she'd saved its life, but the truth was, it had saved hers. No-one could ever call it a second quality dragon.